SAVING LONDYN

BROTHERHOOD PROTECTORS YELLOWSTONE
BOOK NINE

ELLE JAMES

TWISTED PAGE INC

Dedicated to my parents for a great childhood. We didn't have a lot of things, but we had a lot of love!
Elle James

AUTHOR'S NOTE

Visit ellejames.com for more titles and release dates
Join her newsletter at
https://ellejames.com/contact/

SAVING LONDYN

BROTHERHOOD PROTECTORS
YELLOWSTONE BOOK #9

New York Times & *USA Today*
Bestselling Author

ELLE JAMES

CHAPTER 1

"Mother, I don't need a bodyguard." Londyn Tyler-Lovejoy balanced her cell phone against her shoulder as she slapped her cowboy hat against her thigh. The movement was more out of irritation than the need to shake the accumulated dust loose. She was hot and sweaty and wanted a shower.

"Sweetheart, you can't be looking over your shoulder all the time," her mother, movie star Dana Tyler, said. "You have a job to do. The director doesn't have the time or budget to backfill his lead and reshoot scenes if you're incapacitated because some fool is bent on sabotaging your part."

"I can handle it," Londyn insisted. "It's only a little graffiti on my trailer. The set crew was quick to scrub off what they could and paint over the areas that couldn't be cleaned with soap and water."

"I'm not so concerned about the graffiti," her

mother said. "I'm worried about the props that were tampered with. The ladder rungs in the barn scene didn't fail on their own, and the brakes on the Jeep didn't just quit working... They were cut."

Londyn pinched the bridge of her nose. "You heard about those?"

"Yes, I did," Dana said. "You need someone to take charge of your safety, so you don't have to think about it."

"Bodyguards cost money." Londyn gripped the cell phone and straightened her neck. "I took this job to save, not spend."

"You should sell the ranch," her mother said. "Or let me handle the back taxes and late mortgage payments."

Londyn shook her head, even though her mother couldn't see her do it. "No. It's my responsibility now that Gramps is gone. You made it perfectly clear you wanted nothing to do with your old home when Gramps was alive. Why do you care now?"

"Because I see how it's wearing on my only daughter," her mother said, her voice softening. "That ranch will use every bit of your youth and energy, and for what? A pittance of a living—or worse. You'll be working at other jobs to pay the bills."

"I love LJ Ranch," Londyn said. It's my home, and I refuse to take any of your money. Now that the place is mine, it's up to me to make it work. That's the only reason I agreed to audition for this part and then agreed to do the film."

"I don't know why you care," Dana said. "It's just an old ranch with broken-down buildings and fences that always need mending. I never should've let you live with my father for so long."

"So, you'd rather I'd lived in your house in L.A. with the nanny of the week to see you maybe two or three times a year?"

"I did have a busy schedule, but Howard was there," her mother argued.

"Only on the nights he wasn't staying with his secretary." Londyn sighed. "Letting me live with Gramps was the best thing you ever did for me."

"I'm not so sure," her mother said. "You wouldn't be so stressed now if you had stayed in L.A."

Londyn snorted. "I can't imagine living in L.A. now. I love living on the ranch. I wouldn't fit in with the glamorous types you run with."

"I bet you would," Dana said, "if you gave yourself the chance."

"I don't want that life, Mother. I never have."

Londyn had been six when she'd spent her first summer with her grandfather. After a rocky transition from city to ranch life, she'd learned to love the wide-open spaces and her cantankerous grandfather.

Her heart squeezed hard in her chest. Gramps had been the rock in her life. The one person she could count on.

Her mother had always been on a set somewhere else in the world. Howard, her husband for five years, hadn't been interested in raising Dana's child and hadn't had much to say to Londyn on the rare occasions he'd been around.

Londyn's mother might not have sent her to live with Gramps had she not been at her wit's end after the sixth nanny had quit in the middle of filming the movie that was her most important part to that date. It was the movie that shot her to stardom.

She'd had to take a couple of days off the set to deal with Londyn. After interviewing several nannies who'd been much like the former six who had quit, she'd swallowed her pride and begged her father to take Londyn for the summer.

Summer had turned into fall, fall into winter, and twenty years later, she'd still been living on LJ Ranch. Life had been perfect until Gramps had been thrown from his horse, suffering a head injury. He'd refused to go to the doctor, insisting it was nothing.

Two hours after the fall, he'd been dead. Epidural Hematoma. The same injury that had claimed the life of actress Natasha Richardson, or so her mother had informed her.

Gramps had left a letter of instruction in his safe should he die. In that letter, he'd said to contact Ben Standing Bear, the owner of the neighboring Bear Tracks Ranch, for help. She'd done as her grandfather had asked.

Ben Standing Bear had come immediately, promising to help her through spring branding and culling, along with his own workload.

Londyn's mother had returned to LJ Ranch for the first 'time since she'd left twenty-six years before to be with Londyn at Gramps's funeral. After the graveside service, she'd stood at Londyn's side as they'd received condolences from friends and neighbors.

When Ben Standing Bear had stepped in front of them, Dana had turned as white as a sheet and swayed as if she might faint.

At the time, Londyn had chalked it up to the stress of losing her father. Now, she wasn't sure.

At the ranch house, her mother had tried to talk Londyn into selling the ranch, insisting it was too much for one woman to handle. Her insistence had triggered in Londyn the anger stage of grief. She'd told her mother there was no way in hell. She'd rather die than let the family ranch go. Her mother had left the next day.

Once the dust had settled and the initial shock of her grandfather's death had waned, Londyn worked day and night with Ben Standing Bear to get through the spring season typical of cattle ranching. Not until that effort had been completed had she had time to review her finances, only to discover her grandfather had depleted his savings to zero and had taken out a loan, using the ranch as collateral to see her through college and to build a new barn after the old one had burned to the ground.

He'd missed several mortgage payments and owed money on taxes. An official letter in the mail stated the ranch would be foreclosed if she didn't pay up. Another letter from the IRS stated that her property would be seized if she didn't pay the back taxes.

Her mother had called to check on her when she was at her lowest. Londyn had spilled her guts. When her mother had offered to help, she'd refused, stating she'd figure it out. Somehow.

Two days later, her mother had called, saying she had an opportunity for her that would help her out of her financial situation. All she had to do was audition for the lead in a movie that would be filmed in Yellowstone National Park, practically in her backyard. She was a sure win for the part, given her experience riding horses.

She'd responded immediately with a resounding, *Hell no.*

After her mother had patiently explained how much she could make if she got the part, she'd had to rethink her response. In the one film, she could earn enough to pay off the mortgage, the back taxes and have enough left over to put in the bank for hard times, which always had a way of coming around in the business of ranching. Not to mention the residual royalties that would continue to come for the lifetime of the movie.

She'd swallowed her pride and flown to California to audition. Her mother had gone over the portion of the script to be used in the audition and gave her tips on how to project emotion.

"Most of all," she'd said, "be your tough but bighearted self. The main character in this story could be a replica of you. She's tall, beautiful and Native American."

Fate and her Native American looks had played a hand in her audition. Within days of returning to Montana, Londyn had received an offer. Her mother's agent reviewed the offer, asked for minor changes and urged her to accept the offer.

Now, she stood in a hastily built barn, brushing Butterscotch, her buckskin mare, which she'd insisted on using for the riding scenes. "Mother, I have to go. I need to get to my trailer, shower and dress for the scene to be filmed tonight."

"Sweetheart, I know you don't want to consider a bodyguard, but I talked with a friend of mine, Sadie McClain. Her husband has the best security agency in the country. He's sending one of his agents to you as we speak."

"Mother—"

"At least talk to the agent. Let him tell you what he can do to ensure your safety," her mother pleaded. "Please. Just give him a chance."

"I'm not promising anything." Londyn patted Butterscotch and turned to leave the barn. "Gotta go."

"Just give him a ch—"

Londyn ended the call and pushed open the barn door.

As she stepped out into the bright, late-afternoon sunshine, she was immediately surrounded by a crowd of people.

As if on cue, they started chanting, "Go home, Hollywood." Several protestors held up signs that read *GET OFF SACRED LAND.*

Londyn frowned. To get to her trailer, she had to wade through the crowd blocking her path.

She tried to move forward, but a barrel-chested man with high cheekbones and long, straight black hair planted himself in front of her, his arms crossed over his chest. "You don't belong here. None of you belong here."

"We had permission to film here, granted by the National Park Service," she said.

The man shook his head. "This land is sacred to the Shoshone. You disrespect the land and our ancestors by being here."

Londyn opened her mouth to tell the man to move when a voice sounded over her shoulder.

"That might be so but take it up with the film's producers and the National Park Service, not with Miss Tyler-Lovejoy," a deep voice said from behind Londyn.

Londyn turned to stare at a broad chest. Her gaze rose to take in a pair of green eyes. Though not

SAVING LONDYN

barrel-chested like the man blocking her path, this guy's shoulders were broader and just as intimidating, if not more so. The jagged scar that stretched from the corner of his right eye across his cheek did nothing to detract from his ruggedly handsome face.

"Excuse me, should I know you?"

The corners of his lips twitched. "Nash Nelson. Dana Tyler sent me." He held out his hand. "I'm your new bodyguard."

She ignored his hand, her eyes narrowing. "I told my mother I don't need a bodyguard. You can go back to wherever you came from." Londyn turned back to the man standing in her path and lifted her chin. "Please, move."

The man didn't budge.

Londyn sidestepped in an attempt to go around the big Shoshone.

He matched her move.

Nash tapped her shoulder. "May I?"

She rolled her eyes and stepped backward, allowing Nash to take her place in front of the belligerent behemoth.

When Londyn started around the Native American, the man tensed, ready to block her yet again.

Nash met the man's gaze with an intense one of his own and the slightest shake of his head. He didn't have to say a word.

The Shoshone didn't move an inch as Londyn

11

circled the two men and pushed her way through the crowd, heading for her trailer.

The chanting grew louder.

Someone shouted, "You should know better as one of our own!"

Londyn glanced toward the voice. "Tala?"

The beautiful Shoshone woman lifted her chin. "Londyn."

"I thought you moved to Washington when you signed on with Congresswoman Lightfeather."

"I did. But I heard Hollywood was trespassing on sacred Shoshone lands. Color me surprised when I found out you were the lead in the film. Why are you doing this when you know it disrespects those who came before us?"

Londyn shook her head. "The story is worth telling, and the crew has promised to be sensitive to the people and history of the lands."

"But will they?" Tala shook her head. "Already, they've been to the local bars and started fights."

Londyn's brow dipped. "I hadn't heard about that."

"Because you're too busy being a bigshot actor. What happened to the girl who never wanted to leave Montana or your heritage on the LJ Ranch? What would your grandfather think of what you're doing?"

Londyn's lips pressed together. "He'd be proud that I didn't give up on our family's land." She lifted her chin. "Now, if you'll excuse me, I have to get ready for my next scene."

Tala shook her head. "You're not who I thought you were."

"My circumstances have changed, but I haven't." She strode past Tala, her heart pinching hard in her chest. Had she changed? Was she a sellout?

Nash moved around her and used his body as a shield, making it easier for Londyn to maneuver through the crush of protestors.

She squared her shoulders and moved up to walk beside him. "I don't need a bodyguard," she muttered.

"Maybe not," he said. "But your mother hired me. I'm just doing my job."

"It's a waste of your time and mine."

"Your mother warned me you might resist the idea." His lips twisted. "You'll find that I don't give up easily."

"I could file a restraining order," she suggested.

"You could. It would be easier and less expensive if you just talked with your mother," he said.

Londyn snorted. "You don't know my mother."

"Until she releases me from this job, I'm here to provide for your security."

"Great," she said. "I have to navigate through the entire Shoshone Nation camped out on the set, not to mention tripping over a glorified babysitter." She grimaced. "Lucky me."

As she approached her trailer, she smiled. "Just to be clear, my trailer is off-limits."

He nodded. "Understood. However, I need to check it before you enter."

"Check it?"

He nodded. "Someone might pick the lock and lie in wait for you to go inside."

Londyn stopped in mid-stride. "Seriously? It's not like I'm a bigshot movie star or anything."

"No, but you've been the target of several attempts on your life."

"I wouldn't call them attempts on my life," she hedged.

"Then what would you call cut brakes and ladder rungs?" he asked.

"Warnings?" She shook her head. "Whatever." Londyn waved toward the trailer. "Go ahead. Check it. But make it quick. I'm due back on set in an hour and need to get a shower, eat my first meal of the day and be ready for makeup."

Nash pulled what looked like a thick metal pen out of the pocket of his leather jacket and stretched it from six inches to thirty-six in a telescoping move. From his other pocket, he retrieved a mirror and affixed it to the long metal stick.

"What's that for?" she asked.

"To check the undercarriage of your trailer," he said.

"For what?"

"For anything that shouldn't be there," he said. "Now, please stay back."

"Staying," she muttered. "Go. Do your thing. But fair warning... I will have that talk with my mother. Don't get comfortable. This might be the shortest job you ever have as a bodyguard."

"We'll see." Nash moved forward with his mirror on a stick.

Londyn stood back, checked her watch and tapped her booted toe impatiently. Thankfully, the crowd of protestors had moved on to surround the director and the camera crew, leaving Londyn relatively free of their noise and animosity.

She studied the man walking slowly around her trailer. Despite her determination to be rid of the guy as soon as possible, his scar intrigued her. "So, what's your story? Have you always been a bodyguard?"

"No," he responded and disappeared around the back of her trailer.

"What were you before you became a glorified babysitter?" she called out.

"Military," he said from somewhere behind the trailer.

That could explain the scar. He could have gotten it in combat.

He rounded the right side of the trailer and came back into view, his gaze on the mirror.

"What branch?" she asked. "Navy?"

He paused, his brow forming a V over his nose.

ELLE JAMES

"No?" She crossed her arms over her chest. Did he have something against the Navy? "Air Force?"

"Fuck." Suddenly, he dropped the mirror on a stick and raced toward her, shouting, "Get down!"

Stunned by his sudden change of direction, Londyn froze.

Nash plowed into her like a linebacker going in for a tackle. As his body slammed into hers, an explosion lifted them off their feet and flung them several feet through the air.

Londyn landed on her back, her head hitting hard enough that her vision blurred.

Nash landed on top of her, forcing what little air was left in her lungs out with a whoosh.

She lay completely covered by the big man, her ears ringing, unable to breathe or make sense of what had just happened.

As her vision cleared, Nash leaned up on his arms, his hips still pressing hers into the earth. "Are you okay?"

She opened her mouth, but nothing came out. With no air in her lungs, her vocal cords wouldn't work. Her eyes widened.

"What's wrong?" Nash's frown deepened. "Can you breathe?"

She shook her head.

Nash covered her mouth with his and blew air into her, forcing her lungs to expand, reminding them how they should work.

16

When he lifted his head, she released the air in a rush and coughed. "What...the hell...happened?"

He rolled off her, sat beside her and tipped his head in the direction of her trailer.

Londyn pushed up on her elbows, her ears still ringing. Her heart dropped to the pit of her belly as she took in the twisted metal and fiberglass littering the ground where her trailer had once stood.

She looked from the wreckage to the man beside her, his leather jacket torn in several places and several cuts bleeding on the back of his neck and hands. If he hadn't taken the time to "check" her trailer...

What the ever-loving-fuck was happening? She hated to admit it, but her mother had been right to send help.

"Still think you don't need a bodyguard?" Nash asked softly.

Londyn's lips pressed into a tight line. "I'm willing to reconsider."

CHAPTER 2

"FROM WHAT I could see before it went off, it was plastic explosives with a timed detonator pressed into it," Nash said to the sheriff and his deputies who had responded to the 911 call.

Within twenty minutes of the explosion, the movie set had been inundated with emergency vehicles, fire trucks and a news helicopter.

Several protestors had received minor injuries from flying debris and were being treated by the first responders.

The evening sun had sunk below the horizon, cloaking the wild Wyoming landscape in darkness, except for the floodlights positioned around the set, blinding at some points and casting long shadows at others.

Nash had refused their care, more concerned about keeping an eye on his client, Miss Tyler-Lovejoy. She stood with the director, a reporter and a news cameraman, a blanket draped over her shoulders. Every so often, she'd lift her head, her eyes shifting back and forth as if searching the crowd. When her gaze connected with his, she held it like she'd been looking for him.

"Why exactly were you looking beneath the trailer in the first place?" the sheriff asked.

"I was hired to protect Miss Tyler-Lovejoy," he said.

"Were there other attempts on her life that made protection necessary?" the sheriff asked.

"I was told there were two other incidents that raised suspicion," he answered, his gaze holding Londyn's.

The sheriff frowned. "Why were these incidents not reported?"

"You'll have to ask the director and Miss Tyler-Lovejoy. I wasn't here when they happened."

"Does Miss Tyler-Lovejoy have any enemies, disgruntled ex-boyfriends or employees who would wish her harm?"

"I don't know. You'll have to ask her. I just met the woman today." And almost lost her within the first thirty minutes on the job.

His pulse raced, and his stomach roiled at the thought of what would have happened if he'd backed down when Londyn had said she didn't need a bodyguard. She'd have walked right up into that trailer that now lay in twisted pieces. She would have been like the trailer...scattered across the ground.

The recurring flashback of his last mission in Afghanistan blasted through his mind. Of the grenade that had landed less than twenty feet in front of him. Of, Waterson, his battle buddy, throwing himself over the grenade to save the rest of his squad.

Though the temperature had dropped below fifty with the sun's setting, Nash broke out in a sweat, his heart pounding, his breathing labored as if he'd run a mile uphill at full speed.

Every time the flashbacks happened, he was thrown back into that moment, and his body reacted the same fucking way, leaving a burning, ragged mess in the aftermath.

This time, he couldn't afford to succumb to PTSD, the panic attack, or whatever the therapists wanted to call it. He had to remain focused on his charge, or she'd end up like Waterson...her body scattered in pieces across the ground.

Nash clenched his fists and forced himself to concentrate on the present, pushing the memories to the back of his mind. He squared his shoulders. "Sheriff, if you're finished with the questions, I still have a job to do."

"Of course," the older man handed him a business card. "If you think of anything else, call, day or night. I'll answer. This is serious. We can't have someone going around the county planting explosives. We might have more questions." The sheriff closed his notebook and tucked his pen into his pocket. "How long are you in this area?"

Nash's jaw tightened, his gaze pinning Londyn's. "As long as it takes."

The woman might not have wanted a bodyguard, but after what had happened, she was stuck with him until they figured out who was behind the attacks, and he neutralized the bastard.

In a warzone, that meant taking the guy completely out of the gene pool by shooting the coward.

Nash had to remind himself he wasn't in a warzone, though it sure as hell felt like one. After a quick glance around, he shook his head. And it looked like one.

As part of his Brotherhood Protectors onboarding meeting with Stone Jacobs and Hank Patterson, they'd reminded him he wasn't in a warzone. The enemies weren't Taliban or ISIS rebels. They were civilians like he now was. As such, they were all governed by civil law. A man was innocent until proven guilty. He couldn't shoot first and ask questions later—not that he'd done that on active duty.

The briefing had left him feeling a little hand-tied. What did he have to do? Let the enemy throw the first punch, fire the first bullet or blow up his client before he could fight back?

Fuck that. He'd figure out the rules of engagement, but not at the risk of losing his client. If she was in trouble, he'd do everything in his power to protect her, preferably before she was shot, blown up or anything else.

"We have to cordon off the area around the explosion until the state crime lab can get someone in to inspect the damage," the sheriff said. "We have a bomb-sniffing dog checking the other structures before we can let anyone back in."

Nash left the sheriff and crossed to where Londyn was surrounded by the press and other members of the film crew. He didn't like how close they were to her. If one of them was responsible for the explosion, what was to keep him from trying another means of attack? As close as they were, any one of the men surrounding her could easily stab her with a knife.

Nash shoved his way through the ring and emerged next to Londyn.

"We can't shut down production for even a day," the director was saying. "Every day of this effort costs thousands of dollars."

"Some of our equipment was damaged," one man said.

The director waved a hand. "Then get replacements."

"That takes time," the man said.

"Overnight it, kluge together parts from other equipment, hell, do whatever it takes." The director paced back and forth, his head down, his brow furrowed. When the others didn't move, he glared at them. "Between this delay and the protestors, we're bleeding money like a sieve. Do I have to do your jobs for you?"

"No, sir," several men said.

"We have a scene to shoot in fifteen minutes." The director flung his hands toward them. "Go!"

People scattered, leaving Londyn standing next to the director. "My costume for the next scene was in my trailer."

The director shoved a hand through his hair. "What do you want me to do about it? See the costume designer."

"She was injured in the explosion," Londyn said. "She left with the ambulance."

"Fuck!" the director exclaimed. He ran his hand through his hair. "It's the scene where Layla's getting ready for bed. What was the costume?"

"A silk camisole and matching bottoms," Londyn said.

"Surely, one of the females in the crew has something close to that?"

Londyn shook her head, her lips twitching. "They came with flannel PJs. We're in Wyoming. It gets cold at night."

He flung his hands in the air. "So, we'll do the scene sans clothes."

Londyn's head jerked back, and her cheeks filled with color. "Naked?"

Nash frowned. He could tell by the shocked look on her face that Londyn was not happy about the idea.

"Yes, yes, naked." The director looked at her. "And do something about the dirt on your face and the grass in your hair." He turned. "Makeup!"

"Mr. Haynes." Londyn touched the man's arm. "My contract states no nude scenes. Any nudity was to be handled by a body double. She's not due here for a couple more days."

Director Haynes crossed his arms over his chest. "I went out on a limb to bring you onto this project. One nude scene won't kill you."

Londyn's hands tightened into fists. "I didn't sign on for nude scenes."

The man stepped up to Londyn and went nose-to-nose with her. "You'll do it or pack up."

Nash pulled Londyn back and stepped up to Haynes. "The lady isn't required to do nude scenes according to her contract. She almost lost her life in that explosion, she has no place to go to clean up, and you haven't had the decency to ask if she's all right. I suggest you get a grip and come up with an alternative."

Standing a good six inches over Director Haynes, Nash didn't have to do much to intimidate the man.

Haynes blinked up at Nash. "Who the hell are you?"

"Miss Tyler-Lovejoy's bodyguard," Nash said.

The man looked around Nash to Londyn. "Who authorized a bodyguard? We don't have money in the budget for bodyguards for the talent?"

"Don't worry," Londyn said. "You're not paying for it."

"Good." Haynes tugged at the lapels of his jacket. "Keep him on a leash. We can't have him getting in the way." His eyes narrowed. "Were you injured in the explosion?"

Londyn's lips rose briefly. "No. Thanks to Nash. He saved my life by keeping me from going into my trailer."

Haynes stared up at Nash. "Is that right?" His lips twisted. "Good. Glad to hear that. As long as he isn't adding to my budget and doesn't get in the way, he can stay."

Londyn lifted her chin. "What about the costume? I'm not shooting nude."

"Fine," the director said. "Do the scene in your goddamn underwear." He cocked an eyebrow. "Do you have any objections to that? It's no more revealing than wearing a bikini. Surely, you don't object to that. Please tell me you wear under-garments."

"I do." Londyn gave the man a brief nod. "I can do that."

"Good, then get cleaned up and over to makeup. We shoot in..." he glanced down at his watch, "ten minutes." Haynes strode off, shouting instructions to the camera crew.

Londyn shook her head at Haynes's departing figure.

Nash stared down at her. "Are you all right?"

She pressed her palms to her ears. "I'm fine, though my ears are still ringing."

"That'll fade with time."

"I hope so. It's irritating as hell." She gave him a crooked smile. "Though it could be worse." She touched his arm. "Thanks for saving my life. And I'm sorry for being so..."

"Rude?" he suggested.

She chuckled. "I was thinking of a different word."

"Cantankerous," he said with a cocked brow.

She shook her head. "Not that one."

He tried again. "Obstinate?"

Londyn tipped her head. "I was thinking more along the line of bitchy."

"I wasn't going to go there," he said with a grin. "It rings too much of judgment."

For the first time since he'd met the woman, she smiled. "Right answer."

His grin faded. "Did the sheriff question you about possible suspects?"

Londyn's lips thinned into a straight line. "He did.

26

Other than protestors, I couldn't think of anyone who knows me enough to hate me."

"Your mother mentioned that you inherited a ranch from your grandfather," he said. "Was someone else in line for that property?"

She snorted. "Only my mother, and she has no desire to ever live there again."

"Would she want the money from the sale of the land?" He held up his hands. "Not that I'm accusing her of trying to kill you, especially since she hired me to protect you."

"She'd rather die than move back to Montana. She has enough money and doesn't need the money a sale of the ranch would bring."

"What about a rival actor?"

She shrugged. "Everyone has been nice to me on the set. I haven't been in the acting business long enough to make anyone mad that I can think of. I just want to get through this and get back to my ranch."

Nash's brow dipped low. "What about an ex-boyfriend or jealous ex-lover?" Something tightened in his gut, and he found himself holding his breath, waiting for her answer.

Londyn snorted. "I don't have time for a boyfriend and haven't had a lover since..." She blinked. "Hell, since college. That's years ago." Her brows twisted. "I've been busy working the ranch."

"There has to be someone who has it in for you." He pushed a hand through his hair, oddly relieved and tense at the same time. "Since your trailer was targeted for graffiti and demolition, and the props that were tampered with were the ones you were supposed to use, you're clearly the target."

Londyn stared at the mess left by the explosion. "I'll think about it. You're right. I'm the target. I just don't have a clue why." She stared at the people milling around, and her eyes narrowed. "Unless it all has to do with trespassing on sacred lands. Excuse me. I need to talk with someone."

She took off toward the cluster of protestors standing in the shadows.

Nash hurried to keep pace with Londyn.

"You don't have to follow me everywhere, you know," she murmured.

"Yes, I do," he said. "I can't protect you if I'm not near you."

"True." She shot him a glance. "Stay close but let me do the talking."

He nodded.

Londyn stopped in front of a woman with long dark hair, much like hers. "Tala, are you all right?"

The woman she'd called Tala turned to her and gripped her arms.

Nash tensed, ready to step between the two women at the first sign of danger.

"Oh, Londyn, I'm fine, and I'm so glad you're okay." She pulled her into a hug. "That was your trailer. You could've been inside it when it went up." She leaned back. "What happened?"

Londyn's eyes narrowed. "Should I be asking you? Or one of your crowd of protestors?"

Tala shook her head, her eyebrows forming a V over the bridge of her nose. "What do you mean?"

"The explosion wasn't an accident," Londyn said.

Tala looked from Londyn to Nash and back to Londyn. "I don't understand. I thought maybe a gas leak caused it."

"It was deliberate." Londyn tipped her head toward Nash. "Tell her what you saw."

"Someone set explosives," he said. "If Miss Tyler-Lovejoy had gone into that trailer a minute before..."

Tala's eyes widened. "Seriously? Who would do such a thing?"

Londyn's lips pressed into a thin line. "Tala, how upset are the Shoshone over the movie crew being on sacred grounds?"

The woman pressed her hands to her chest. "You don't think we had anything to do with it, do you?"

"There have been a number of incidents on the set," Londyn said. "One of which was graffiti on the back of my trailer that said, *Go Back Where You Came From.*"

"When was that?" Tala asked.

"Last night," Londyn answered.

"We didn't get here until this afternoon." Tala shook her head. "We had nothing to do with it. We didn't even organize until this morning." She looked around at the others in her group. "Ours is a peaceful protest. No one is armed—especially not with dynamite or whatever they used to destroy your trailer." Tala touched her arm. "We don't like the movie crew tromping all over sacred grounds, but we wouldn't kill anyone over it. Especially not you."

"Londyn, darling," a woman called out from behind Nash.

He turned to find a dark-haired woman wearing a flowing white dress hurrying toward them. A tall, blond-haired man dressed in jeans, chaps, a leather vest and a cowboy hat followed her.

The woman rushed past Nash and flung her arms around Londyn. "Oh, thank God you're all right."

Londyn awkwardly patted the woman's back and then stepped out of her embrace. "I'm fine. I take it you and Craig weren't injured in the blast?" She looked past the woman to the man in the cowboy hat.

"I was in my trailer, studying my lines, when the blast practically threw me out of my chair," the woman said.

"I was getting into my costume for the night scene," the man said. "My trailer shook so hard my blow dryer fell off the counter." He stepped past the woman and pulled Londyn into a crushing embrace. "When I heard it was your trailer, I was worried about you and came over as soon as I could get through the crush of emergency personnel."

Nash frowned at how long the man was holding Londyn. He stepped forward and gripped the man's shoulder. "Hey, man, let her breathe."

The man stepped back, his arm still around Londyn's waist. He cocked an eyebrow at Nash. "And you are?"

"Your worst nightmare if you don't take your hands off Miss Tyler-Lovejoy."

Londyn shook her head. "Nash, I've got this." She looked up at the man she'd called Craig. "I'm fine. You can let go."

He pulled her back into his arms, crushing her to his chest. "I'm worried about you."

Nash snorted. "So worried, it took you twenty minutes to make your way over to her?" His hands clenched into fists.

"Law enforcement herded us out into the open and wouldn't let us get closer," Craig said. "We were told to stay put while they questioned people and ran the bomb-sniffing dogs through." The man held tightly to Londyn. "I wanted to come, but they wouldn't let me."

Nash wouldn't have let anyone stand between him and someone he cared about. They'd have to shoot him to make him stay away. "Right," he said with a grunt. "Very heroic."

Londyn glared at Nash but directed her words to the man holding her. "Let go of me, Craig."

"You're my leading lady," Craig said. "What would've happened if you'd been injured or killed?"

"Haynes would find another leading lady," the woman beside Londyn said.

Londyn reached behind her, grabbed Craig's thumb and twisted his arm around and away from her body.

"Hey, hey!" Craig cried. "Ease up, or you'll break my thumb."

Londyn's mouth turned up on the corner as she held onto the man's thumb. "That's the idea. Save the love scene for the camera." She let go of Craig's thumb and waved a hand toward the man and woman. "Nash, this is Craig Ryland and Julia Banes, also known as 'the talent.'"

"I'm the lead male, and Lana's—" he tipped his head toward Londyn, "love interest in the movie." He rubbed his thumb with a frown. "We'll have to work on the chemistry."

Londyn turned to Nash. "And this is Nash Nelson, my—"

"Boyfriend," Nash said and held out his hand to Craig.

Londyn's eyes widened briefly, but she didn't call him out on his lie.

Craig reached for the hand to shake.

Nash gripped the actor's hand hard enough to make the man flinch. "Nice to meet you, Mr. Ryland."

He released the man's hand and offered his hand to the woman. "Miss Banes."

Julia gave him a weak handshake and released it quickly.

"I just arrived today," Nash said. "And it seems I'm just in time." He slipped an arm around Londyn and pulled her up against him.

She stiffened but didn't twist his thumb like she had Craig's.

"How terrible that you could've been caught in the explosion with Londyn." Craig shoved his hand into his back pocket. "Well, I'm glad neither of you was hurt. Will you be on set for the next scene?" he asked Londyn.

"I'm headed that way now," Londyn said.

"Good." Craig nodded. "Haynes likes to keep on schedule,"

Julia glanced from Nash to Londyn. "Nothing makes him crankier than delays."

"Believe me," Londyn murmured. "I want to finish this job—the sooner the better." She hooked her hand through Nash's elbow. "Come on, boyfriend. I need to get moving before the big, bad director blows a gasket."

Nash let her lead him to the cabin on the edge of the movie set. Camera equipment was set up all around the front of the cabin, and lights were trained on the porch.

Director Steve Haynes emerged through the

cabin's front door. "We need Lana in place ASAP." The man's gaze searched for and found Londyn as she approached with Nash. "There you are." His brow dipped low. "You're not ready."

"She'll be ready in a minute." A woman rushed forward with a hairbrush.

Nash stepped away.

Another woman came at Londyn with what looked like a makeup palette.

While Londyn stood still, the woman with the hairbrush worked quickly and efficiently, brushing the tangles, dirt and grass from her hair.

The one with a makeup palette whipped out a soft brush and applied just enough makeup to cover the smudge of dirt on Londyn's face and to enhance her eyelashes, cheekbones and lips.

Once they'd completed their work, they melted into the shadows.

"The crew's inside, ready to go when you are." He turned to Craig Ryland. "Mount up. You'll ride in on my cue."

Ryland nodded and strode to the edge of the floodlights, where a man held the reins of a black horse.

Londyn's lips twisted. She shot a glance toward Nash. "You can't go in with me."

He frowned.

"I'll be fine," she said. "This shouldn't take long.

I'm just inside for a few minutes and then come rushing out to defend my ranch."

"Has anyone checked the cabin for explosives?" he asked.

Haynes nodded. "The sheriff had a bomb-sniffing dog run through the set and around all the other trailers. We're clear. Apparently, the only affected trailer... Well, you know."

"Was Miss Tyler-Lovejoy's." Nash's jaw clenched.

"If you want to stay," Haynes said to Nash, "you'll have to hang back behind the camera crew and stay quiet while they're filming."

Londyn nodded. "Go."

Nash hesitated another minute, not liking that she wouldn't be in sight. He didn't trust that the crew would look out for her, but he didn't have a choice. He moved back behind the camera crew and took a stance, ready to race forward should she need him.

Director Haynes ducked into the cabin.

For the next fifteen minutes, he waited. While he waited, he texted Swede, letting him know what had happened and asking him to locate lodging for Miss Tyler-Lovejoy for the night since her trailer had been destroyed. Swede promised to get back to him as soon as he had something.

Voices sounded inside. Haynes emerged, glanced left and right, nodded and yelled, "Action!"

Everyone grew silent as the cameramen focused on the cabin.

Movement sounded from inside the cabin.

Haynes, standing at the edge of the set, motioned toward Craig, who was seated on the black horse. The man dug his heels into the animal's flanks.

The horse bolted forward at the same time as Londyn burst through the doorway carrying a rifle and wearing nothing but her bra and panties.

"Cut!" Haynes shouted.

Craig yanked back on the reins.

The black horse reared.

Craig slid out of the saddle and landed hard on the ground.

People stood back while the horse reared again, whinnying excitedly.

Londyn stepped forward as the animal came down on all four hooves.

Nash was halfway to her when Londyn snagged the bridle.

The horse reared again, lifting Londyn off the ground as she held on tightly to the leather straps, speaking softly, insistently.

When the beast dropped back down, Londyn kept talking, her voice soothing.

The handler who'd been working with the horse rushed forward, causing the frightened animal to skitter sideways.

"I've got this," Londyn said firmly. "Back off."

The man stepped backward as members of the

crew grabbed Craig off the ground and carried him to safety.

Londyn kept talking to the horse until his nostrils stopped flaring, and he stood still.

She ran her hands over his forehead and along his neck, speaking to him in a soothing tone.

Nash eased up behind her and ran his hand along the opposite side of the horse's neck. "Want me to take him?"

Londyn shook her head. "No. He's going to be fine. He just wasn't ready to stop running when Craig pulled back on the reins."

"That horse is impossible," Craig said from the sidelines.

"It's not the horse," Londyn whispered. "Is it, Reggie?" she murmured as she scratched behind the animal's ear.

The horse tossed his head as if in agreement.

"That's right," she said softly. "You're beautiful and not used to working at night with someone who doesn't know the first thing about handling a creature as magnificent as you."

"Where's our stuntman?" Haynes called out.

"Here," said a man dressed exactly like Craig as he stepped up beside Londyn. "I'll take Reggie from here." He took the reins out of Londyn's hands and led the horse away.

"Everyone in place," Haynes called out.

"You have to get back," Londyn said. "We're about to shoot the next sequence with the stuntman."

"Why? What's he going to do?"

"You'll see," she gave him a nudge toward the cameramen. "I think this is the last shot for the day—if we get it right on the first take."

Nash backed into the shadows of the camera equipment and crew, his brow furrowed. He wasn't sure he could protect this woman in such a chaotic and fluid environment.

The man who'd taken the reins from Londyn led the horse back into the shadows and mounted.

The animal danced sideways for a moment, then settled.

Londyn grabbed the rifle from where she'd dropped it on the ground.

"Ready?" Haynes called out.

Londyn nodded and went back into the cabin.

"Ready," the man on the horse called from the shadows.

"Action!" Haynes commanded.

Londyn burst through the door with her rifle as the man on the horse shot out of the shadows, racing straight for Londyn.

Nash started forward.

The man on the horse leaned down, grabbed Londyn's free hand and swung her up, rifle and all, landing her across his lap in the saddle. Then he nudged the horse, and it raced out of sight into the darkness of night.

Nash didn't wait for Haynes to yell, "Cut!" before he ran after them.

He caught up with them a few yards later as the stuntman lowered Londyn to the ground.

She stood barefoot on the cold, hard ground, her arms wrapped around her chest in the cool night air.

Nash removed his leather jacket and draped it over her shoulders. "Are you all right?"

She nodded, a shiver shaking her entire body. "I am. Thanks."

He rubbed her arms in an attempt to warm her. "Is that it?"

She shook her head. "I don't know. The director might want to run the scene again."

Nash shook his head but didn't say anything. Instead, he pulled her close, wrapping his arms around her.

She stiffened against him.

"I'm just trying to keep you warm," he said. "Don't feel the need to twist my thumb. It's just me doing my job and protecting you."

"From what?" Londyn shivered again.

"Hypothermia," he answered. "You can't stand out in the cold for long."

"I'll stay as long as it takes to get the scene right." She turned in his arms and stared out at the camera crew.

Haynes and the cameramen had their heads together next to the camera, replaying the video. After a long moment, they all backed away.

"It's a wrap," Haynes said. "See you all in the morning, bright and early."

"You can go?" Nash asked, his lips against her ear.

She nodded. "Yes. But the big question is to where?"

Nash's cell phone vibrated in his pocket. The text from Swede made him smile. "My team has you covered."

"How so?" she asked.

"We have a cabin in Yellowstone National Park."

"We do?" she asked, her brow furrowing. "Since when?"

He grinned. "Since now. Are you ready to go?"

She looked toward the area where her trailer had been. "My purse, driver's license and truck keys were in my trailer."

"You'll ride with me. I'll have my team work on getting replacements for all those things. For now, let's get you somewhere you can get a shower and some sleep."

She frowned. "Isn't it too far to drive each day?"

"I'll get you there and back in time. Given what happened earlier, I think you'll be safer away from the set."

Londyn sighed. "You're probably right. And right now, I'm too tired and cold to argue."

"Good. Then come with me."

"Let me grab my clothes," she said.

Nash walked her to the cabin and checked inside before he allowed her to enter.

The cabin was empty. Members of the crew were either gone or stowing equipment for the night.

Londyn entered the cabin, went to an antique cupboard against the far wall and fished her clothes out of the bottom drawer.

She shrugged out of Nash's leather jacket.

Nash turned away, allowing her a modicum of privacy as she dressed.

Once she was done, she joined him. "You want your jacket back?" she asked, handing it over to him.

He shook his head and draped it over her shoulders again. "I don't need it right now."

She pushed her arms through the sleeves and wrapped the excess around her. "Thanks."

She shivered again and fell in step beside him as they left the cabin.

When they reached a black pickup parked beside the other vehicles in the grass on the opposite end of the camp, he opened the passenger door and held it for her as she climbed inside.

Londyn fumbled with the seatbelt until Nash took over, securing it over her lap. Still leaning over her, he stared into her eyes. "It's going to be okay."

She gave him a crooked grin. "I hope you're right. If I didn't need this job, I'd be tempted to tell you to keep driving and take me as far away from here as we can get."

"I can take you anywhere you want to go," he said as he straightened.

Londyn shook her head. "Part of me wants to take you up on that offer."

"But?" He cocked an eyebrow.

She stared straight ahead, her chin lifting. "When I leave this set, this production, it will be on my own terms, not with tail between my legs scared of some asshole too cowardly to show his face."

Nash closed the door and rounded the front of the truck to slide into the driver's seat. Londyn was nothing like the women he'd known. He'd arrived expecting the tedious task of protecting a diva incapable of taking care of herself. Instead, he'd found an independent young woman with a gorgeous body and a stubborn streak that might just get her killed.

His eyes narrowed as he shifted into drive and pulled out of the parking area.

His assignment had almost ended as soon as it had started. Fortunately, he'd managed to keep the woman from dying on his first day. She might not have wanted a bodyguard, but he'd already saved her once. And once you saved someone, you were morally, ethically and superstitiously responsible for that person's life in perpetuity.

At least, that was how Nash felt. Until the threat

was neutralized, this stubborn, headstrong woman was his responsibility.

One thing was certain.

Guarding Londyn was going to be a lot more difficult and dangerous than he could have imagined.

CHAPTER 3

Londyn must have fallen asleep less than a mile away from the film location. She didn't wake until the truck pulled to a stop and engine noise ceased.

A door opened and closed, then the door beside her opened, allowing a waft of cold air into her warm cocoon.

Lyndon blinked her eyes open.

"Hey, sleepyhead," a deep voice spoke softly beside her. "We're here."

She lifted her head and peered out the front windshield.

The headlights shined at a small log cabin with a homey front porch.

Her brow wrinkled. "Where's here?"

"At a cabin on Yellowstone Lake."

She frowned, laced her hands behind her head and stretched her back. "I'm staying here?"

Out of the corner of her eye, she could see him nod. "Yes, ma'am."

"Please, call me Londyn," she said. "I'm not old enough to be a ma'am, and Miss Tyler-Lovejoy is too much of a mouthful."

"Yes, ma'am—" He grinned. "Londyn."

"I really need to do like my mother did and change my last name to Tyler. It's so much simpler." She sighed. "But that takes time and money—both of which I seem to be short of lately."

Nash stared up at her, tilting his head. "I'd carry you in, but something tells me you might resist this idea."

"You'd be right." Londyn turned to face the man who'd saved her from the explosion, noticing, not for the first time, how ruggedly handsome he was, even with the jagged scar across his right cheek. Having been in LA with her mother on more occasions than she preferred, she'd been around handsome men. Most often, they were trouble. Egotistical, selfish men who were more interested in what you could do for them than what they could do to actually help another human.

Working on and now owning a ranch, Londyn had never had much time, nor would she in the near future, to nurture a relationship with a man.

Most of the men she knew worked on her ranch or neighboring properties. Having a relationship with someone working or living that close would open her up to complications should the relationship go sour. As early as getting her first training bra, she'd made it a rule not to get into an intimate relationship with any of the ranch hands or ranch owners of adjacent spreads. She liked the simple ranch life and refused to make it more complicated than it had to be.

She dropped her arms and fished at her side for the seatbelt buckle. Once she found it, she popped the buckle loose and let the belt retract on its own. "How long was I out?"

"Thirty-five minutes," he answered.

She nodded, shoved her hair out of her face and swung her legs around. "I have to make sure I get to the set early tomorrow morning. The director has no patience for lateness."

"I'll be sure to get you there at whatever time you need to arrive," he promised.

As Londyn slid out of her seat, her feet missed the running board.

Nash's hands caught her around the waist as she pitched forward and slammed into his chest.

For a long moment, he held her there. Then he eased her to the ground.

"Thanks," she said, heat rushing up into her cheeks. "I'm not usually so clumsy."

"No worries. I'm here to protect you."

"From someone trying to hurt me," she said,

pulling his leather jacket close around her. "Not from my two left feet."

His hands left her waist, but one remained on her arm to steady her in the gravel. "I'll provide any form of protection you need while I'm on the job." He waved his hand toward the cabin. "My guy Swede got us the last cabin available."

"Well, thanks." She looked up at the cabin. "Does this place have running water, a soft bed and warm blankets?"

"That's what I'm told." He grinned, transforming his battle-scared face into something special.

Londyn's heart skipped several beats and then raced to catch up. She had to force herself to look away from the man or risk falling into his sexy brown eyes.

"I must be more exhausted than I thought," she murmured to herself.

"Then let's get you inside, through the shower and into bed. I'm sure Haynes has a full day of filming for you tomorrow." Nash reached into the truck's back seat, grabbed a duffel bag, slung it over his shoulder then came to stand beside her.

"Ready?"

She nodded.

He rested his free hand lightly against the small of her back and guided her up the wooden steps. Once on the porch, he dropped the duffel bag and fished his cell phone from his pocket. He switched on the flashlight and handed it to Londyn. "If you can hold that, I'll get this lock opened."

Standing close enough to the man that she could smell his aftershave, Londyn held the cell phone over his hands, the light shining down on the combination lock box. He smelled so good it was affecting her senses, causing her pulse to quicken.

Nash rolled the four numbers one at a time, then pulled on the box. It opened. A shiny silver key lay inside. He fit the key into the door lock, twisted it and pushed open the door. When he reached inside with one hand and flipped a switch, soft light filled the one-room, compact cabin.

"You can have the first shower," Nash said as he stepped inside and held the door for Londyn.

She stared into the cabin, her feet firmly planted on the wooden planks of the porch. "Is this your cabin or mine?"

His lips twitched. "Swede was only able to secure one cabin. It's yours. But if you don't mind, I would like to make use of the shower."

She frowned. "If there's only one cabin, where are you going to sleep?"

"I have a sleeping bag in my truck," he said. "I'll sleep on the porch."

Londyn shivered at the thought of the man sleeping on the porch. "Do you realize how cold it gets at night?"

He nodded. "I'm familiar with this area of the

country. I grew up near Whitefish, Montana. My bag is rated for extreme cold weather. Come in off the porch. I'll check the place out, then it's all yours."

Her eyebrows rose as she stepped through the door into the cozy room that served as a living room and kitchen, all in one. A large, overstuffed leather sofa took up most of the space in front of a potbellied stove. Beyond the sofa was a kitchenette with a tiny stove with two burners, a refrigerator, a sink and a small table with two chairs.

Nash closed the door behind her and twisted the lock. Then he crossed the short distance to the only other door in the room and disappeared inside. He was back out three seconds later. "Clear." He stepped past her, his shoulder brushing hers, and opened the door, grabbed his duffel bag, dropped it on the floor beside the sofa and turned back to the door. "I'll get my sleeping bag out of the truck. Make yourself at home." He left through the door, closing it softly behind him.

Londyn passed through the narrow door on the far wall into a bedroom with barely enough room for the queen-sized bed, a single nightstand, a small chest of drawers and a little closet. Another door led into a tiny bathroom with a toilet and a shower-tub combination. Fresh towels hung on a rack near the shower curtain.

Sore and dirty from the explosion and the layers of makeup and hair product they'd used on her,

Londyn couldn't think of anything she'd like better than a long, hot shower.

She stepped into the bathroom, closed the door, and turned on the water in the tub. After she adjusted the temperature and rerouted the water to the showerhead, she stripped out of the clothes she'd worn all day and kicked them to the side.

Tired and aching, she stepped over the side of the tub and stood beneath the spray, letting it run over her hair, face and shoulders, the heat soothing her aching muscles. After several long minutes beneath the healing waters, she looked around, realizing she'd brought nothing with her but the clothes on her back. Thankfully, there were travel-sized bottles of shampoo and conditioner in the cubby and a small box with a bar of soap. Not knowing how big the water heater might be, she quickly washed her hair, face and body, then applied conditioner and rinsed the remaining dirt and dust from her body. The water was still warm when she turned it off and reached for one of the towels on the rack beside her. She patted her skin and hair as dry as she could and wrapped the towel around her.

Londyn stared down at the dirty clothes on the floor, wondering if they would dry by morning if she washed them in the sink that night.

A soft knock on the door made her hands tighten on the towel tucked around her. She had to remind herself Nash was a stranger to her, yet here she was, practically naked in a bathroom that didn't have a door lock. "Yes?" she said, looking around for something she could use for a weapon and finding nothing.

"You might want this." Nash opened the door a crack and stuck his hand through. In it was a faded black T-shirt and a pair of royal blue boxer briefs. "It's the best I can do for the night. I have a pair of sweats you can wear to the set tomorrow. If you let me know your sizes, I can see what I can have brought in."

She took the proffered offering, touched that he'd thought about her predicament and had come up with a temporary solution to running around naked in nothing more than a towel. "Thank you."

He shut the door. "Swede had the kitchen stocked with some supplies. Hungry?"

Her belly rumbled loudly.

Nash chuckled. "I'll take that as a yes."

Londyn pulled the boxer shorts up her legs, feeling oddly sexy in the smooth fabric. Knowing he had worn these at some time made it seem even more intimate. Heat rose up her neck into her cheeks and coiled low in her belly. She quickly pulled the T-shirt over her head. The jersey fabric slid over her skin, the hem falling to the tops of her knees.

Her nipples puckered against the soft material.

Londyn ran her hands over her body, shocked at its response to wearing men's clothing. No. It wasn't that they were men's clothing. They were Nash's, and they held the lingering scent of the man's cologne like he'd stored it amongst his clothes.

What was wrong with her? She'd had several attempts on her life in the past forty-eight hours. Yet, she was fantasizing over the man whose clothing caressed her body. A man she'd just met—also, the guy who'd saved her from a certain explosive death.

That had to be it. She had some hero-worship complex going on since he'd saved her.

She tried to finger-comb her hair to no avail and ended up wrapping it in the towel. The stylist in charge of her hair would have to sort through the tangles tomorrow. Without a brush, she could do little to straighten her long black hair. Not for the first time in the past few years, she wondered why she didn't just cut it off. Short hair made much more sense for a rancher as busy as she was.

Then again, her hair was part of her heritage. Though her mother had never told her who her father was, it was obvious to everyone she looked like him, not her blond-haired, blue-eyed movie star mother.

When she was with her mother, no one ever guessed they were related.

When Londyn had been old enough to ask about her father, her mother had said he wasn't in the picture. He'd been her drunk, one-night stand on her last night in Montana before she'd moved to California to pursue a career in film. She hadn't known his name and didn't think she'd ever see him again to let him know he had a daughter.

She'd discouraged Londyn from looking for the man, saying he was probably a roughneck who worked on a pipeline and had a woman in every town he visited. And if he did come looking for Londyn, it would be to see how much money he could get out of her mother now that she was a wealthy movie star. According to her mother, men only came looking for their bastards if there was money in it for them.

Londyn only took her mother's words halfway to heart. She didn't believe all men were assholes. Her grandfather had been a stern man, but he'd had a big heart beneath his tough exterior. Deep down, he'd been heartbroken when his only daughter had left Montana and refused to return. Only on his deathbed had he opened up enough to say they'd had a disagreement over his daughter's choice of boyfriends.

Since her mother had married three times and divorced three times, Londyn guessed her mother had left that boyfriend behind in Montana, having revenge sex on her way out.

Until Londyn had moved to Montana to live with her grandfather, she'd never known what it was like to have a father figure in her life. Especially one who gave a damn about her.

In her grandfather's gruff way, he'd loved her and taught her how to treat people by example. He'd always been fair but never a pushover. He'd helped people who needed it but who'd been willing to help themselves. And he'd instilled in her a love of the land, the animals and all the good that hard work could achieve.

Based on her dark hair, eyes, skin and bone structure, Londyn was obviously of Native American descent. She'd always wondered what tribe she belonged to. One Christmas, her grandfather had gifted her a DNA testing kit. When her mother had found out about it, she'd blown a gasket, demanding Londyn throw it away.

To keep the peace and save her grandfather a lot of grief, Londyn had told them both she'd tossed the kit in the burn barrel. But she'd lied. She'd already sent in her sample. She'd beat her grandfather to the mailbox every day for a month until the results had come back.

The results had showed that she was primarily of Shoshone descent. When she'd gone to college in Bozeman, she'd joined the American Indian Council of MSU, eager to learn more about her people.

That had been where she'd met Tala and other young people eager to make a difference in the lives of their people. The only difference was that the others had come primarily from the surrounding reservations, while Londyn had lived on a ranch with her white grandfather. She'd never told them who her mother was. She'd liked the relative anonymity her mother's choice of shortening her name had provided.

Standing in the bathroom, dressed in Nash's clothing, all those memories raced through her head. She looked as Native American as the kids from the rez. Had her mother warned him that her daughter didn't look anything like her? Had he been shocked that she was Native American instead of the blond, blue-eyed beauty her mother still was?

With the towel balanced on her head, Londyn squared her shoulders and pulled the door open.

What Nash thought of her was irrelevant. She didn't need his approval for anything. The man was only there to do a job.

Protect her.

So far, he'd proven himself adept. Who brought a mirror on an extension rod to a movie set when you're assigned to guard a movie star?

She shook her head, a smile playing on her lips at the absurdity of the mirror and the fact that she was far from a movie star. Hell, she was a completely unknown actor, more comfortable in the saddle than on a film set.

When she emerged from the bedroom, her body was enveloped in delicious warmth.

Nash turned from tossing a small log into the fire inside the potbelly stove. He smiled and pointed to the cell phone he had balanced between his chin and shoulder. "Let me put you on speaker." Nash took the phone in his hand, punched a button and spoke, "Swede, say hello to Londyn Tyler-Lovejoy."

"Hello, Miss Tyler-Lovejoy," a deep male voice said.

She stared at Nash and shook her head. "Hi. Thank you for all you did to get me into a room tonight."

"Glad to help," Swede said. "I'm sorry about your trailer and your belongings. Did you have a good insurance policy?"

Londyn snorted. "Hardly. The trailer belonged to the production company. At least I'm not out that cost. I need to make a run up to my ranch to collect additional clothing to get me by while I'm on set in Wyoming."

"Could we send someone over to get what you need?" Swede asked. "It might be faster for someone from our headquarters here in Eagle Rock to swing by to get what you need rather than for you to leave the set in the middle of filming."

Londyn snorted softly. "I appreciate the offer, but it's weird having strange men going through my underwear drawer."

Swede laughed. "I hadn't planned on going through anyone's drawers. Hank Patterson's wife, Sadie, volunteered to go to your ranch with him if you want her to get some things for you. She'd like to drive down to Yellowstone and see what's going on because she's familiar with movie production and all."

"Is she?" Londyn asked. "How so?"

Swede chuckled. "Ever hear of Sadie McClain?"

Londyn's eyes narrowed. "The name's familiar."

"Do you go to the movies often or stream them online?" Swede asked.

"I've seen a few. I'm new to the movie industry and haven't met many actors except the ones on this set. I've spent most of my life ranching. We don't have much time to go to the movies or watch much television, except during the winter."

"Then you might not be familiar with one of Hollywood's biggest stars. Sadie McClain is one of the most sought-after actors in the business."

"Sadie McClain..." Londyn shook her head.

"Look her up. You might recognize her face," Swede said. "But she's all female. If you don't want her to go to your ranch, she can pick up what you need on the way down from a store in Bozeman."

"I guess it would be all right for her to stop at my ranch. My neighbor, Ben Standing Bear, is pulling double duty between his place and mine while I'm on location filming. I can give him a call and let him know Sadie and Hank are stopping by for me."

"Good. I'll let Hank know he and Sadie are a go to deliver whatever you tell them you need," Swede said. "I was just about to fill Nash in on what I learned from the sheriff's office, Wyoming Highway Patrol and the state crime lab folks investigating the explosion."

"We're listening," Nash said as he stirred the fire and closed the door. Heat radiated from the small stove, warming the room. "They figure out who set those charges?"

Londyn moved closer to the source.

"Not yet," Swede replied. "The sheriff questioned the man in charge of the pyrotechnics for the movie. He maintains strict control over what they have. He showed the sheriff his supplies and his inventory tracking application. Everything was accounted for. I called one of my contacts in the Wyoming Highway Patrol. One of the mining companies near Yellowstone reported missing inventory two days ago. One of their employees stole some C4 from their supplies and a couple of detonators. They have the man in custody."

"Was he the one who set the charges on my trailer?" Londyn asked.

"They don't think so. He said he sold the items to someone behind a bar in West Yellowstone."

"No name?" Nash asked.

"No name," Swede confirmed. "And the man's face was covered in a black ski mask."

Londyn frowned. "Two nights ago, production came to a halt because the props we needed for the next five scenes had been destroyed in transit an hour away from delivery. Our director gave everyone half a day and night off. Almost everyone piled into their cars and headed to West Yellowstone for a buffalo burger and beer." She met Nash's gaze. "They went to the Buffalo Bar and Grill. Was that the bar where he made the sale?"

"That's the one," Swede said.

"Does that mean a member of the crew has an issue with me?" Londyn shook her head. "I don't remember making anyone particularly angry. I work hard and try hard to get scenes right the first time."

Nash laid a hand on her shoulder. "We don't know if it's someone on the crew. There aren't many places in the area to blow off steam. The Buffalo gets a lot of people from all over."

Londyn looked up into his gaze. "I don't believe in coincidence, do you?"

He hesitated before sighing. "No. I don't."

"That means any person on the set who went to the bar that night could be my attacker." Londyn turned and padded barefoot across the tile floor, turned and came back to the stove. "That gives me zero confidence in my safety on the set."

"I'll be there."

"But will you be close enough to make a difference?" Swede asked.

Londyn shook her head. "They make him stand behind the camera crews."

"I can be with you everywhere else except when they're shooting," he said.

"We have a lot of riding scenes coming up. That will put a lot of distance between us," she said.

"Are you riding alone or with other riders?" Nash asked.

Her brow wrinkled as she thought through the next few pages of the script. "With other riders."

"Could I be a spare rider with no lines?" he asked.

Londyn canted her head to one side. "Can you ride?"

He smiled and nodded. "I was raised on a ranch. I learned to ride before I learned to walk."

She touched a finger to her chin. "That might work. I'll speak with the director tomorrow. He's already on a tight budget, so he might not be able to pay you."

Nash shook his head. "That would be double-dipping. I'm already being paid by Brotherhood Protectors to provide for your safety."

"Yes, but you announced yourself as my boyfriend," she said.

"A concerned boyfriend would work for free to take care of his girl." Nash took her hands in his. "Got anything else for us, Swede?"

"No," he said. "The sheriff provided me with the names of all the people on the set, movie production crew and protestors. I'm running them through crime information databases to see if I find a match. I'll let you know if I get any hits."

"Thanks," Nash said.

"Let Hank and Sadie know I appreciate their offer to run by my ranch," Londyn said. "It's got to be way out of their way."

"Not if you go by helicopter," Swede said.

Londyn chuckled. "Nice. I won't feel as bad knowing they're not driving all the winding roads to get there and back down here."

"Will do. Send me a list of what you want, and I'll forward it to Sadie," Swede said. "Out here."

"Out here," Nash said and ended the call.

He stared at Londyn. "If you don't mind, I'll get that shower and be out of your hair."

"Speaking of hair, you don't happen to have a brush or comb in that bag of yours, do you?"

He grinned. "As a matter of fact, I have both." He dug inside the duffel bag and handed her a thick brush and a black comb. "If you want me to work the tangles out, I'm pretty good at it. I have younger sisters."

She smiled. "Is there anything you can't do?"

His smile faded. "Lots. But a shower would be nice."

She nodded, stepped out of his way, and waved him toward the bedroom door. "Be my guest. And thank you for the PJs." She waved a hand toward her T-shirt-shrouded body. "It feels good to be in something that doesn't stir up a cloud of dust when you walk through a room."

He grinned. "You wear it better than I do."

She waggled her eyebrows. "If you think the T-shirt looks good, you should see the boxer briefs."

His smile slipped, and his eyes flared. "After you, I'm sure they'll never wear the same."

She frowned and looked down at the T-shirt, picturing the boxer briefs beneath. "My hips are wider than yours, but the shorts are stretchy. I'm sure they'll shrink back."

Nash held up a hand. "It's not that they'll be stretched out of shape. I just won't ever wear them again and not think of who wore them last." He touched a finger to the corner of his scarred eyebrow in a mock salute. "I'm going under. See you on the other side."

He pivoted on his heel, snagged his duffel bag and marched through the bedroom into the bathroom, closing the door firmly behind him.

Londyn's gaze followed him all the way until he disappeared behind the door, her blood pumping hot through her veins, racing to her core where it coiled and flared like a furnace igniting.

Her bodyguard was entirely too hot to be confined with her in the tight space of the cabin. As heated as she felt at that moment, she might incinerate before the night was over.

She was already way out of her depth, acting in a

movie with no previous experience, not even a school play. All her focus needed to be on learning her lines, studying the script and preparing for the next scene.

Seducing the bodyguard her mother was paying for could send her off on the wrong track.

Wrong track, hell.

Nash was the kind of man who could leave her totally derailed.

CHAPTER 4

NASH STRIPPED out of his dusty clothes, noting the rips in the fabric of his jeans and the crusted blood on the backs of his legs and arms. His leather jacket had shielded his upper body from much of the shrapnel generated by the exploding trailer.

They'd been lucky. Had Dana Tyler not told him her daughter was living in a trailer on location, he might not have brought his handy mirror and extension rod.

The day could have ended a lot differently had he backed down when Londyn had told him she didn't need a bodyguard.

The black-haired beauty's stubborn independence was sexy as hell—and had nearly gotten her killed.

He dropped his clothes on the pile of Londyn's clothes she'd left on the bathroom floor, making a note to himself to look for laundry facilities. Since every item of clothing she'd brought with her to the location had gone up with the trailer, she'd need the dirty ones cleaned soon. Hank and Sadie might not make it down to Wyoming for a day or two.

He tried hard to keep his mind from going to the boxer briefs he'd loaned Londyn. He'd never considered them particularly sexy. And he'd never seen them on a woman, and still hadn't, since they were hidden by the oversized T-shirt that hung down to the tops of Londyn's knees. But damned if his imagination wasn't going wild, picturing how the smooth fabric would stretch over the swell of her hips and thighs.

"Fuck," he muttered and turned on the water, twisting it to the coldest setting. Since he wasn't waiting for it to warm, he stepped beneath water the temperature of freshly melted snow. Nash bit down hard on his tongue to keep from yelping as the icy spray pelted his skin, chinking away at the heat that had flared to an inferno the moment Londyn had stepped out of the bedroom wearing his T-shirt, the pebbled tips of her breasts making tiny points protrude from the jersey material.

Watching her running around the set in her bra and panties that evening had been his first glimpse of her slim, athletic body.

Nash had been proud of her refusal to shoot the scene in the nude. Plus, he was surprised at how she'd performed the scene without demonstrating the slightest bit of discomfort at running around in nothing but her bra and bikini panties.

Nash had seen bathing suits more revealing than Londyn's underwear. But the fact they were underwear, not parts of a swimsuit, made the costume that much more intimate, which had to make Londyn, an actress new to the profession, uncomfortable. She'd handled it so well and hadn't hesitated to grab the reins of the spooked horse in an attempt to calm the animal.

Never mind, she was in her underwear and barefooted. The horse could easily have crushed her feet beneath his hooves, knocked her down, and trampled her to death.

He'd rushed forward as quickly as he could to help her without spooking the horse worse.

In the end, Londyn had managed to soothe the horse and keep all ten of her toes, all while standing half-naked in front of at least two dozen members of the production crew.

Once the chilled water had Nash's libido under control, he turned the handle to warm, built a full head of lather in his palm and scrubbed his body from head to toe, careful to clean the crusted wounds on his arms and legs. They stung for a second, but these superficial wounds were nothing compared to the ones he'd sustained when the grenade had taken his friend Waterson's life.

Those wounds were more than physical. The

shrapnel had been painful going in and equally painful when they'd been surgically removed at the field hospital prior to shipping him to Germany and the hospital at Ramstein.

The plane that had flown them back for medical care had also carried the body of the man who'd given his life to save his team. Only Waterson wasn't on a stretcher, surrounded by medical personnel working to keep him alive. He'd been in a body bag, headed to his final destination.

Nash's heart raced, and his breathing grew ragged as the memories rushed back at him. In an effort to push them back, he scrubbed harder, as if the friction, soap and water could wash away the memory of his friend's shredded body.

"Breathe," he said softly. He drew a deep breath, held it and then let it out slowly. Willing his frenetic movements to slow, he smoothed soap over his body in slower, soothing motions.

He repeated the deep breathing until his pulse slowed to a regular rhythm, and his thoughts returned to the cabin, the shower and the woman warming by the fire in the next room.

He wasn't in Afghanistan. Though the explosion that day had been too much like what had happened that last mission, everyone had survived —including the one person he'd been sent to protect.

He lifted his face to the water and rinsed, anxious

to get back to the other room to assure himself that Londyn was still safe.

After shutting off the water, he quickly toweled dry and pulled on clean jeans. His anxiety eating at him, he yanked open the door and strode through the bedroom into the living area, barefoot and carrying his T-shirt.

Londyn straightened from spreading what looked like his sleeping bag out on the sofa, her eyes widening as her gaze hit his naked chest.

He frowned and pulled the T-shirt over his head. "I'm sleeping on the porch. Why is my sleeping bag in here?"

She shook her head. "You realize you're in bear country, right?"

He shrugged. "I'm a light sleeper, and I have a gun. I'm not worried about it."

"Well," she said. "I am worried about it. You might be a light sleeper, but I wouldn't get any sleep, knowing bears like to visit these cabins because careless tourists leave trash out that attracts them. They come looking for it." She pointed to the sofa. "I'll sleep better knowing you're not being eaten by a hungry bear."

His lips twitched. "A hungry bear wouldn't eat me."

She crossed her arms over her chest, making the T-shirt rise up her thighs and giving him a peek at the royal blue boxer briefs she wore beneath it.

Nash's pulse leaped, and his mouth suddenly dried. He tried to swallow but couldn't. That little bit of royal blue had him instantly tied in knots.

She cocked an eyebrow. "You'll sleep on the sofa?"

Though he knew it was a mistake, he could do nothing more than nod.

Her face softened. "Good. I need sleep so I don't look like I've been ridden hard and put up wet for the shoot tomorrow."

"You'll look amazing." His brow dipped low as he realized she still wore the towel on her head. "The brush didn't work for you?"

Londyn shrugged. "I started to pull the tangles out but wanted to get you set up first. I figured you couldn't argue much if I had it all situated before you came out." She reached for the brush. "I'll work on it now. If you don't mind, I'd like to stand near the fire while I do it. It's the toastiest place in the cabin. Since the explosion, I can't seem to get warm enough. It shouldn't take me too long."

"You're probably still in a bit of shock." He walked back into the bedroom, grabbed the extra blanket off the foot of the bed and returned to the living room. He folded the blanket in half and laid it on the floor between the potbellied stove and the sofa.

"Sit," he ordered.

She dropped onto the blanket and pulled her knees up to her chin, fitting the big T-shirt over her legs. When she pulled the towel off her head, he took

ELLE JAMES

it from her hands, laid it on the floor beside her and held out his hand. "Brush."

She glanced over her shoulder, her brow furrowing. "I need it to get through the snarls."

He plucked the brush from her hand. "Let me."

Her brow twisted. "Are you sure? My hair is really thick. The tangles can be stubborn."

"Like you?" he said with half a smile. "Don't argue. Relax and enjoy the warmth."

She turned her head back to the fire. "See for yourself."

Nash started at the ends, easing the brush through small sections of hair until he had all the knots out of the bottom four inches. He moved up, working the knots out a little at a time without yanking or ripping the hairs out by the roots.

As Nash worked, Londyn's shoulders relaxed. She closed her eyes and let her head fall back. "That's nice," she murmured. "How many little sisters do you have?"

"Three," he said. "Though they're not so little anymore. The youngest is in college, studying to be a speech pathologist. The middle sister works as a financial analyst in Seattle. The oldest is the mother of twin five-year-old boys. Her husband works for the Forestry Department, and she teaches English to high school students."

"Any brothers?" Londyn asked.

"No. Just sisters." He chuckled. "My father and I

70

were outnumbered." Nash continued working the tangles from her hair until it lay smooth and straight, falling halfway down her back. He didn't want to stop, but he'd finished and had no excuse to keep stroking the brush through her hair. "All done."

Londyn ran her hand over her hair. "I can't remember the last time anyone brushed the tangles out of my hair. That was nice. Your sisters must have loved you."

"They do. And I love them." He pushed to his feet and walked into the kitchen. "Mom worked full-time as a physical therapist. By the time she got home, she was tired. We had to help with dinner and dishes and then get ourselves through showers and homework. We all pitched in." He pulled deli meat out of the refrigerator, along with mustard and mayonnaise, and set them on the counter. "Is a sandwich all right with you?"

"I'd love it." She rose and joined him in the small kitchen barely big enough for one person, much less two.

Every time he turned, he bumped into her or brushed against her breasts. His groin tightened.

"We have lunch meat… Is there any bread?" she asked as she opened one cabinet door after another.

"I thought I saw a loaf in here." Nash opened the cabinet beside the refrigerator, where he found the bread. He laid it on the counter with the meats and condiments.

Londyn produced two plates, a knife and two glasses.

"Mustard or mayo?" he asked.

"Both."

He nodded. "Right answer." He slathered a generous layer of mayo on one piece of bread and mustard on the other and laid them on the plate.

Londyn layered deli meat over the mustard side, a slice of cheese over the meat and topped it with the bread with the mayo.

Once they had both sandwiches complete, they each took a plate.

"Table or in front of the stove?" Nash asked.

Londyn was already halfway to the stove.

He grinned. "Stove, it is."

She settled on the blanket in front of the stove and sat cross-legged with the plate in her lap.

Nash sat beside her, lifted his sandwich and took a bite.

"So, how did you end up being in charge of brushing your sisters' hair?" Londyn asked and took a bite of her sandwich.

Nash chewed and swallowed before answering. "Since I was the oldest, I was responsible for helping my little sisters. None of them liked Mom brushing out their hair. She loved us all dearly but was busy getting everything ready for the next day and didn't take the time to ease the tangles out of their hair." He took another bite of his sandwich.

"But you did," Londyn said. "What a nice thing for a brother to do. Most guys wouldn't have done it."

He shrugged and swallowed. "There was a big age gap between us. I was the product of a high school pregnancy and her first marriage that didn't even last until I was born. My sisters were half-sisters from Mom's second marriage to my stepfather."

"You were close to them?" Londyn swept her tongue across the mustard on her bottom lip.

Nash almost forgot what they were talking about. He had to replay her words in his head to get his mind off the mustard on her lip. "Being older, I kind of felt like I was responsible for them. Like a second dad."

Londyn turned to face Nash. "What about their father? Was he not helpful?"

Nash smiled. "My stepfather was the dad he didn't have to be for me. I was seven when he married my mother. He knew he was getting a package deal and accepted me as his own from day one."

"You're lucky," Londyn said softly. "Most men aren't as willing to raise another man's child." She took another bite of her sandwich.

"He was all in. He taught me how to throw a football, bait a hook and filet a fish. He taught me how to treat a woman by the example he set with my mother," Nash stared down at the sandwich in his hand, the memories of his childhood washing over him, making him smile. "He was a warrant officer in the

Army. Though we didn't have much money, he made sure my mother got the college education she'd always dreamed of. And he didn't stop loving me when his daughters were born." He nodded. "I was lucky. I had a great childhood because of him."

Londyn stared at the potbellied stove, chewing on the bite of sandwich in her mouth. After she swallowed, she said, "I had a great childhood once I moved in with my grandfather. I wasn't cut out for life in Hollywood. I didn't look like the glamorous people who floated through. My mother married a few times. Her husbands didn't want anything to do with me, and my mother was always on location somewhere in the world, leaving me with a nanny."

"I'm sorry."

"Don't be," she said with a smile. "When the last nanny quit because I was too precocious, my mother sent me to live with my grandfather on his ranch in Montana for the summer. I never moved back to California."

Nash polished off the last bite of his sandwich and set his plate on the end table behind him. "Did you miss your mother?"

Londyn nodded. "I did. She missed me, but I didn't fit in there, and she knew it. Plus, she had a career that required her to travel to different locations, sometimes all over the world. She couldn't take me with her, and I made it hard for her to leave me with a nanny. Living with my grandfather was the perfect answer. I loved the ranch life and thrived in Montana." She took another bite and set her plate on the table behind her.

"If you love ranching so much, why take up acting?"

She sighed. "My grandfather died three months ago. He'd mortgaged the property to put me through college. Drought and harsh winters hit him hard, and he couldn't keep up with the property taxes. I didn't know any of this until he fell off his horse and died of an aneurysm."

"I'm sorry," Nash said softly.

Londyn's eyes welled with tears. "Yeah. Shit happens. Thing is, my grandfather was often grumpy and would snap at you when you did something stupid." She snorted. "But I loved that grizzled old cowboy, and I love living in Montana with the big skies, mountains and pastures that stretch for miles." Her voice faltered, and she blinked several times.

Nash felt her pain and wanted to put his arms around her and hold her through it all. Instead, he remained silent, letting her have the time to pull herself together.

Londyn squared her shoulders, breathed in deeply and let it out. "I had to do something to raise enough money to save the ranch. Mother knew this script needed someone who looked like me and could ride a horse. It was a perfect fit if I could act as well. With some coaching from my mother, I auditioned, did a screen test and got the job. If I can make it through the entire production, I can pay off the debt. From there, I'll figure out how to make the ranch pay for itself."

"That's a lot for one person to manage," Nash said.

Her jaw tightened. "I have a couple of loyal ranch hands, and my neighbor stepped in when my grandfather died to help me through the spring roundup, culling, and tagging. I just need to come up with the money to keep the bank or the government from seizing the ranch."

"What about your mother? Couldn't she help you?" Nash asked.

Londyn shook her head. "I refuse to ask her for money. She wants me to sell and move to LA. I can't do that." She stared at the cast iron stove in front of her. "I don't belong there. I don't fit in. My life is in Montana, not California."

"I get it," Nash said. "I've been in cities where you drive for a long time before you can get out of it like it won't let go of you without a struggle."

She looked at him, her eyes wide. "Yes. That's exactly how it feels. Out here, I step outside my house and can breathe without inhaling exhaust fumes. Instead of horns honking and the constant roar of traffic on the move, I hear the chirp of cicadas, the occasional bellow of a cow looking for her calf or a hawk's cry. It's beautiful." She gave him a crooked smile. "Sounds silly, but that's how I feel. The bottom line is that I'm not a city girl."

"What if this movie launches you into stardom?"

Londyn grimaced. "I hate to say I'd never do it again. It all depends on how well the ranch is performing. I don't want to lose it. It's a part of me."

"You realize they'll require you to be there for film screenings and premiers, don't you?"

She nodded.

"They'll have to advertise the movie with you and the lead male showing up for the red-carpet events and on talk shows. That will keep you away from Montana quite a bit."

Londyn's lips pressed together. "My mother mentioned all of those things. Yes, I'll go for the premiers and show up for interviews." She yawned. "I'm just not good at stuff like that. What good does it really do?"

"It gets the word out about the film and increases ticket sales," Nash said. "The more sales they make, the more royalties you earn. And if this movie is well-received, I'm betting the studio will want you to do more movies."

Londyn pinched the bridge of her nose. "On the one hand, the money would be beneficial in allowing me to make some improvements on the ranch, but it sounds like a commitment I'm not sure I want to make." She shook her head. "Right now, I'm focusing on my primary goal...to keep my ranch."

"Sorry. I didn't mean to spin you up when you should be getting rest." He ran his gaze over her. "Any lasting effects from the explosion?"

Londyn rolled her shoulders. "I'm a little stiff, but that could be from this evening's horse scenes." She smiled. "At least my ears aren't ringing anymore." Londyn yawned. "I guess I should leave you to your sleeping bag and go to my room. Thanks for getting the fire going. I finally warmed up. And thanks for brushing my hair. That was the best. Your sisters were lucky to have you."

Nash pushed to his feet and held out his hand.

When Londyn placed her palm in his, a spark of electricity raced up his arm, spreading heat through his body. He pulled her to her feet a little faster than was necessary, making her stumble and fall against him.

His arms circled her waist, steadying her.

She rested her hands on his chest and looked up at him wide-eyed, her mouth parting on a soft gasp. Her body pressed to his, and all Nash could think of was that the woman was close enough to kiss.

Nash stared into the inky-black depths of her gaze.

When her tongue darted out to dampen her lips, it drew his attention lower.

Definitely close enough to kiss.

As if drawn to her by an irresistible, magnetic force, his head lowered until his lips were but a breath away from hers. All she had to do was rise up to meet him.

His breath arrested in his lungs, and he froze as if caught in a time warp, willing her to make that move.

Londyn's fingers curled into the fabric of his T-shirt. Her body tensed against his.

For a moment, Nash thought she'd step away. It would be the right thing to do. Because as much as he wanted the kiss, he knew it would change everything.

The voice of reason confined to the very back of his mind begged him to take that step backward, to stop the insanity before it could take firm root.

"This might be a big mistake," she whispered, "but hell—" Londyn rose up on her toes and pressed her lips to his. At first tentative, her mouth brushed his, then pressed firmer, her tongue darting out to breach the seam of his lips.

He opened to her, meeting her tongue with a long and earth-shattering caress.

Her hand slipped up his chest and curled into the hair at the back of his head, holding him tightly, urging him to get closer, to take more.

And he did, one hand pressing against her lower back, the other cupping the back of her head and his fingers slipping into her thick, damp hair.

He kissed her like there might not be a tomorrow for them, like a man consuming his last meal. No matter how close he held her, it wasn't close enough.

When he remembered to breathe, he lifted his

head and stared down into her glassy eyes. "Definitely a mistake," he murmured.

Her tongue swept across her swollen lips as her gaze held his for a long moment. Then she blinked and moved back.

Though he wanted to retain his hold on her, he let his arms drop to his sides.

She ran her hands over her thighs, stretching the T-shirt tightly over her pebble-tipped breasts. "I'm not sure what just happened..."

He knew exactly what had happened and wanted it to happen again. The feeling was so intense that it shook him. "You should get some rest." He moved around her, snagged his sleeping bag and headed for the door.

"Nash, wait," she called out. "You can't sleep outside. The bears..."

"I can handle the bears," he said and stepped out onto the deck. "Lock the door behind me." He pulled the door closed and released the breath he'd been holding. He tossed the sleeping bag on the porch, marched to his truck and retrieved the handgun he kept tucked in the console.

Yeah, he could handle the bears a hell of a lot easier than he could handle himself with Londyn in the room.

CHAPTER 5

LONDYN LAY IN THE BED, her pulse thrumming, heat radiating throughout her body for a long time after that kiss. She gripped the sides of the bed to keep from marching out onto that porch and demanding another kiss to prove to herself it had been an anomaly. Like he'd said, she was still in a bit of shock after that explosion.

She'd never felt as deeply impacted by just a kiss before in her life. It couldn't be real. Could it?

Midnight came and went before Londyn finally fell into a fitful sleep. Only to dream about the man whose kiss had rocked her world so thoroughly, she was certain she'd never be the same.

She woke before the alarm she'd set on her cell phone, before the sun had chased the gray light of predawn from the sky and stretched, groaning at the aches and pains presenting themselves from the previous day's trauma.

She listened for sounds of movement from the room in the little cabin. The silence was only broken by the chirping call of an early bird getting a jump on the day.

Like she should. Since it took over thirty-five minutes to drive to the film location, she needed to get a move on. She knew that when the director cast her in the lead female role, he'd taken a big chance on her. Lead rolls usually went to famous actors with a following that would bring movie-goers to the theater to see them.

Londyn had none of that, and because she looked nothing like her famous mother, playing that marketing angle would have less of an effect.

Thankfully, Craig Ryland was a big name in the industry. From the rumors Londyn had overheard, he'd been paid ten times what the studio had offered her. They were banking on his marketability to make that money back at the box office and more.

He'd be hard to replace at the last moment.

Londyn, on the other hand, had come cheap. If they had to replace her, she figured it would be no big deal. In fact, Julia Banes knew the script. She could wear dark contacts to cover her green eyes and straighten her wavy hair. She didn't have the dark skin and high cheekbones like Londyn, but makeup could hide those facts.

The point was that if she wanted to see this project through and save her ranch, she couldn't give them any reason to replace her, like showing up late on the set and holding up production.

It was bad enough that the attempts on her life had put some kinks in the schedule and caused some crew members to start spreading the rumor that because they were trespassing on sacred ground, the movie was cursed. Bad things would continue to happen until they left Yellowstone to the ghostly ancestors watching over it.

Londyn padded barefoot through the cabin to the front door, praying she didn't find the bloody remains of Nash spread across the porch due to being mauled by a bear.

She shook her head at her morbid thoughts. The noise of a bear mauling would have woken her in the night.

Despite that supposedly reassuring idea, she held her breath as she twisted the lock and pulled the door open.

The porch was empty, the sleeping bag and Nash nowhere in sight.

Londyn frowned and stepped outside.

A cool mountain breeze whipped around her bare legs, raising gooseflesh across her skin. She wrapped her arms around her middle and searched the immediate vicinity for the man who was supposed to be protecting her.

She didn't see any sign of him in his truck, but he could be lying across the back bench seat. Determined to find him, she crossed the porch and was about to descend when a movement out of the corner of her eye made her turn toward the corner of the cabin.

Nash jogged into view, stopped, dropped, and did a burpee. He dropped again and pumped out ten pushups, then leaped to his feet and resumed jogging.

When he spotted her at the top of the steps, he slowed to a stop, barely breathing hard, his skin glistening with a light coating of sweat.

"Good morning," he said. "Ready to head out?"

She shook her head. "How long have you been awake?"

He glanced at his watch. "Forty minutes."

"No unwanted visitors last night?" she asked.

"Just a couple of curious coyotes," he said, his lips twitching. "They were as surprised by my presence as I was by theirs."

Londyn shook her head. "You aren't sleeping on the porch tonight."

Nash didn't argue.

Londyn's eyes narrowed. "You're going to do whatever the hell you want to despite what I say, aren't you?"

He nodded slowly. "I need a shower, then I'll be ready to go."

She led the way back into the house where it was warmer, even though the fire had burned out in the potbellied stove.

Nash crossed to his duffel bag and dug out a pair of heather-gray sweatpants. "Catch," he said. He tossed the pants toward Londyn.

She caught them with one hand. "What do you want me to do with these?"

"I think they'll go great with the boxer briefs," he said with a wink.

Her lips twitched. "Thanks."

"Do you want a different T-shirt?" he asked.

"I assume they're all the same size." Londyn shook her head. "In which case, no. I can make do with this one until I can get the clothes from my ranch or stop at a store somewhere and buy something that fits a little better."

"We can stop by the park gift shop later and see if they have any shirts and sweatshirts," Nash said.

Londyn wasn't a fashionista or in any way particular about her clothes, but not having any was proving to be frustrating. At this point, she would gladly wear a Yellowstone National Park sweatshirt. "That would help since we're not sure when Hank and his wife will head this way."

He snagged a clean T-shirt and a pair of blue jeans from his duffel bag. "I'll be back in two shakes."

Londyn's gaze followed him as he ducked into the

bedroom. If she wasn't mistaken, the man hadn't taken any underwear with him. Were the boxer briefs an anomaly for Nash? Did he prefer to go commando beneath his jeans?

Her heartbeat kicked up a notch at the thought of his naked, fine ass inside the snug denim jeans.

Her lady parts tingled at the thought of slipping her hands beneath the waistband of his jeans and cupping his bare skin.

Londyn threw her hands in the air.

What is wrong with me?

She dropped the sweatpants on the sofa, marched into the little kitchenette and yanked open the refrigerator. "I don't know him from Adam. He could be a serial killer, a mama's boy, or worse." Yet, she was fantasizing about putting her hands down his pants to cop a feel.

Her core heated as the image filled her mind again. "Eggs." She grabbed a carton of eggs and stopped short of slapping it on the counter. She found bacon in one of the drawers. This time, she did slap it onto the counter, finding it strangely satisfying to take her frustration out on a package of bacon.

After she located a pan and spatula, she made quick work of frying the bacon and then cooking scrambled eggs in the bacon grease.

She'd just scraped the eggs onto two plates when

Nash emerged from the bedroom, barefooted and wearing nothing but jeans.

The view of his broad, bare chest sucked the air right out of her lungs. Her hand loosened on the handle of the frying pan, and it slipped free.

Londyn dove to grab it before it hit the floor. Instead of catching it by the handle, she caught the hot pan with her fingers. "Fuck!"

Rather than drop it again, she tossed it toward the sink, where it clattered against the stainless steel.

Nash rushed forward. "Hey, did you burn yourself?" He took her hands in his and frowned down at them.

"It's okay," she said, her left hand turning red where it had connected with the hot pan.

"No, it's not," he said, guiding her toward the sink. "Let's get it under some cool water."

Still holding her injured hand, he turned on the sink water, checked that it was cold and then moved her hand beneath the spray.

Though the water was cool on the burn, having Nash as close as he was and half-naked was making Londyn hot everywhere else but her hand.

Hell, he even smelled good.

She closed her eyes and drew in a deep breath through her nose, letting the scent of the man fill her lungs.

Wow.

No man had the right to smell that good.

"Are you okay?" his voice brought her back to earth.

Londyn's eyes popped open.

Nash was studying her face, his own so close she could feel the warmth of his breath against her cheek.

Heat rose up her neck and filled her cheeks. She snatched her hand away, dripping water across the floor. "Breakfast is ready," she said, her voice tight and embarrassingly squeaky.

He grabbed a dishtowel and reached for her hand. "Let me dry your hand."

She plucked the towel from his grasp. "I can do that. You'll want to eat while the food is still warm."

He frowned but didn't push the issue. Instead, he carried both plates, full of fluffy scrambled eggs, to the small table.

Londyn carried the plate of crispy bacon and sat opposite the man who'd haunted her sleeping and waking dreams, keeping her head down and her gaze on the food.

Knowing she didn't have much time to get to the movie set, Londyn ate in silence, finishing quickly. She carried her plate to the sink, washed it and dried it.

When Nash brought his plate, she held out her hand.

He shook his head. "I can take care of my plate. You should go change."

Londyn hurried away from him and snagged the sweatpants from the back of the sofa where she'd left them. She passed through the bedroom into the bathroom, closed the door and leaned against it. From where she stood, she looked directly into the mirror over the sink, barely recognizing the woman in the reflection.

Her cheeks were a ruddy red beneath the darkness of her skin. She touched her fingers to her lips, which were still a little swollen from last night's kiss. The long, thick hair Nash had so painstakingly brushed was once again tangled and mussed.

However, it was her eyes that stood out. She stared at herself with a confusing combination of fear, anticipation and desire.

Never in her life had she been so disconcerted by a man as she was with Nash. Her instant attraction to him and the rush of desire she'd experienced before, during and after that kiss had thrown her into a spin.

If she wanted to regain control over her life and her emotions, her best course of action would be to avoid Nash altogether.

She ran her hand over the sweatpants, which were slightly worn but super soft. Londyn stepped into them, pulled them up over her hips and cinched them tighter to keep them from falling off. Used to wearing blue jeans, the sweatpants felt too light, more like pajamas than something she should wear to work.

But what choice did she have until her clothes arrived with Hank and Sadie? Hopefully, the costume designers had already completed work on replacement costumes for the ones lost in the explosion. At least the costumes designed for the movie were decent and not something wild and over the top. She might be able to wear them back to the cabin after filming was completed for the day.

Until then, she was glad to have clean clothes to wear to the set.

Londyn tried to finger comb her hair again and gave up. She needed to make a list of items she'd need from the ranch. Besides clothing, a brush would be at the top of the list.

She pulled on her boots, which looked funny with the sweatpants, and left the bathroom.

Nash stood in the living room, looking fresh and gorgeous, his hair damp and neatly combed back. "Ready?"

She nodded and grabbed the copy of the movie script from the counter. "The sooner we leave, the better. I want to be there a little earlier than usual to coordinate with the makeup, hair and the costume folks. Director Haynes doesn't like to be kept waiting."

Nash nodded. "If you have everything you need, we can go."

Her lips curled. "I need a lot of things, but none of them are here."

He dipped his head. "Right. But that will soon change."

"I hope so," she said. "Thanks for the loan of some of your clothes."

"You're welcome," Nash said. "I only wish I had something that fit you a little better."

"I'm grateful for anything at this point," Londyn headed for the door. "I'm ready."

Nash opened it for her and waited for her to pass through before following her out onto the porch. He descended the stairs and led the way to his truck, opening the passenger door for her.

She cocked an eyebrow. "For your information, I'm perfectly capable of opening my own doors."

"I have no doubt." Yet, he stood firm and waited for her to climb up into the truck. "For your information, so were all the women in my family. But I was taught to open doors for ladies and the elderly. It's a hard habit to break, not that I want to break it. I hope it doesn't offend you."

As she settled in the passenger seat, she frowned for a moment and then shrugged. "No. I'm not offended. And perhaps the correct response to someone opening a door for me is *thank you*. I've been out on the ranch for so long that I forget the rules of polite society. So, in the name of good manners, thank you."

He grinned. "You're welcome." He closed the door and walked around to the driver's seat. Once he was settled behind the wheel, he buckled his seatbelt and started the engine.

"Do you want to listen to music?" he asked.

She shook her head and opened the script. "I want to read through my lines. I have a scene with Craig today. He gets annoyed if I forget my lines."

"No problem," Nash said.

For the next ten minutes, Londyn memorized the words she would say to Craig's character in a heated discussion. Her mother had coached her on how to express different emotions subtly rather than hitting the audience over the head with it. She closed her eyes and rehearsed the words in her head. She'd committed to memory most of the scene.

As she worked through the last few lines, her cell phone buzzed in her purse. She pulled it out, read the name on the screen and grimaced. "I'm sorry, but I need to take this call."

"No worries," Nash said, his gaze on the road ahead.

Londyn inhaled and let out a long, slow breath before answering. "Hello, Mother."

"Londyn, darling, what's this I hear about your trailer exploding? Are you all right? Was anyone hurt?"

"I'm fine," Londyn said. "Some members of the film crew were injured, but no one severely."

"Thank goodness," her mother said. "Did they shut down the set?"

"No, Mother. Just the area around the explosion. In fact, I'm on my way to the location now."

"That's wonderful, darling," her mother said. "I'm glad to hear they're not putting the production on hold. A delay like that can kill a project."

"Another explosion like we had yesterday could kill more than a film," Londyn reminded her.

"Absolutely, my dear. I also heard our Mr. Nelson was instrumental in saving you from injury. Was his quick reaction and the fact someone is well and truly targeting you enough to convince you to let him stay?"

Londyn's gaze shifted to Nash, who sat silently behind the steering wheel. "Yes, Mother. I've reconsidered. He can stay until we figure out who's behind what's happening."

"Wonderful, darling," her mother said. "I only want what's best for you. You...kn—love—."

"We're losing signal, Mother." The connection went silent. Londyn sighed and laid the cell phone in her lap. She looked over at Nash. "I guess it's official."

"What's that?" he asked, shooting a glance her way before returning his attention to the road.

"You're staying until the attacker is identified." Her brow furrowed. "That is, if you still want to. I mean, it is dangerous and all."

Nash chuckled. "You do realize I was on active duty, special ops, during a war, right?"

"Yes, but this isn't a war. You're in the United

States. It's not supposed to be dangerous here." She waved her hands in the air. "Things like this aren't supposed to happen."

Nash glanced her way, meeting her gaze. "Why do you think Hank Patterson has expanded his Brotherhood Protectors Organization from Montana to Yellowstone, Colorado, Louisiana and Hawai'i?" He shook his head. "People need protection, even here."

Londyn's eyes widened. "He's got protectors in all those places?"

"Yeah." Nash returned his gaze to the road ahead. "There are bad people everywhere in the world and here at home. That's why I have a job. That's why so many of our former military folks have jobs with Hank's team."

Londyn stared ahead. "I should've stayed on the ranch. There, I only had to worry about wolves, bears, getting thrown by a horse or trampled by cattle. I don't get it. Who would want to kill me?"

"That's what we need to figure out," Nash said. "In the meantime, I'll be with you until we do."

Londyn nodded. "Thank you."

When they arrived at the parking area, Londyn dropped down from the truck and hurried toward the set.

The camera crew, sound and lighting personnel were in place. Craig Ryland and Troy Masters were in position, dressed in their costumes for the scene

Londyn had prepared for the night before and on the ride in.

Julia Banes stepped into the scene, wearing the costume designed for Londyn, her long dark hair hanging straight down her back. Londyn frowned and muttered, "What the hell?"

CHAPTER 6

"WHAT'S WRONG?" Nash whispered.

The actress spoke the lines Londyn had memorized.

"Those are my lines. That's my part." Londyn stopped behind the cameras, fighting the urge to march into the middle of the set and demand to know why Julia was performing her part.

But she refused to look like a spoiled diva. There had to be a good explanation.

As the script called for, Troy grabbed Lana—in this case, Julia—and pressed a pistol to her temple.

Julia dug her elbow into Troy's side, grabbed the hand holding the gun, yanked it down, twisted his wrist and took the gun. When she moved it to her other hand, she fumbled and dropped it in the dirt.

"Cut!" the director shouted.

Londyn hurried over to Haynes. "Hey, Steve, why is Julia playing my part?"

"About time you got here," Haynes said. "We started an hour ago. Where were you?"

"I came at the time we usually start," Londyn said. "When did you change the schedule to an hour earlier?"

"Last night. I let everyone know to show up an hour earlier."

"Apparently, not everyone," Londyn said. "Did you make this change after I left for the evening?"

"Maybe. I don't know when you left." Haynes waved at one of the cameramen. "The angle of that camera isn't quite right. I want to see more of Lana, less of Troy." He turned back to Londyn, his brow furrowing. "I checked the weather yesterday evening. They're calling for storms late this afternoon. You might recall we have the cattle drive sequence today. If we want to shoot that scene, we have to start no later than noon. Which meant moving this take earlier."

"And this news happened after I left?" Londyn asked. "How was I supposed to know?"

"When I made the announcement, someone said they would let you know." He looked around and waved his hand toward Julia. "Julia, I think."

Londyn looked across to where Julia stood talking to Craig. She smiled and laughed at something the actor said. Julia glanced toward the director, her eyes widening. She said something to Craig, then made her way across to where Londyn stood with Haynes. "Oh, Londyn, I'm so glad you got here. We were just practicing the scene until you arrived."

"Steve tells me that you were supposed to let me know about the schedule change," Londyn said.

Julia blinked. "Oh, was I supposed to do that?"

Director Haynes had already walked off to talk to the cameraman.

Londyn's eyes narrowed. "That's what Steve said."

Julia pressed a hand to her mouth. "I'm so sorry. I must not have heard him tell me to do that."

Director Haynes called out, "Where is my Lana? We don't have all day. Get into costume, Londyn."

Londyn cocked an eyebrow toward Julia.

Julia gave her a crooked smile. "You can come change in my trailer since I'll have to find clothes anyway." Julia led the way.

Londyn held back, walking beside Nash.

He leaned down and whispered, "Are you all right?"

Londyn's jaw tightened. "We'll see."

Julia climbed the steps to her trailer and unlocked the door. "I'm sorry for the mess," she said. "I wasn't expecting company." She turned and held the door for Londyn.

Londyn hesitated. "I'll wait here. When you get changed, you can hand me the clothes."

Julia shrugged. "Suit yourself. I'll only be a minute." She ducked inside the trailer and closed the door behind her.

Londyn glanced toward Nash.

His eyebrows rose on his forehead. "Sounds suspicious."

Londyn's lips pressed tightly together. "Hard to say. Yesterday was chaotic. Haynes might not have heard her say that she would get in touch with me."

Nash tipped his head and met her gaze, holding it. "Or she could've conveniently forgotten."

The thought had crossed Londyn's mind. What better way to show the director that she could do the part as well as Londyn, with Londyn out of the way?

"Was Julia up for the same part?" Nash asked.

"I don't know." Londyn hadn't really thought about who else had auditioned for the role of Lana. "I could ask my mother."

"Or the director," Nash suggested.

Londyn shook her head. "He has enough on his mind trying to keep to a schedule, especially with so many moving parts."

Nash nodded.

"Besides, my mother has her finger on the pulse of Hollywood." Londyn snorted softly. "She'd know every name on the list of the women who applied for this part. If she doesn't know, she'll know who to ask. And they'd tell her."

Nash's lips quirked on the corners. "That, I'd believe."

Londyn's lips twisted. "You've met my mother."

"Not in person," Nash said. "But I spoke with her on the phone. She is very...direct."

"That's my mother." Londyn grimaced. "That woman knows exactly what she wants and pursues it singlemindedly until she gets it. That's how she made it so big."

The trailer door opened, and Julia's head peeked out, her shoulders bare except for her bra straps. "They're a little dusty. We were filming the fight scene, after all. I'm sure the dust will come out if you give them a little shake. It's a good thing that you and I are pretty much the same size, or we wouldn't have been able to practice the scene with me in costume."

Londyn climbed the stairs.

As she reached the top, Julia opened the door wider, exposing the fact she wore nothing but her bra and a pair of thong panties. She held out the bundle. Once she handed the wad of clothing to Londyn, she smiled and winked at Nash.

Londyn frowned as she struggled to keep from dropping the items. She was just getting used to the cast showing up wearing less than what her grandfather would have considered appropriate. The fact she'd stood there half-naked and winked at Londyn's fake boyfriend made her hackles raise and her fingers curl like one of her barn cats getting ready to pounce on a rat.

Once she had everything secure, she descended the stairs.

"Are you sure you don't want to change in my trailer?" Julia asked. "I mean, since you don't have a trailer anymore..."

Londyn had forgotten that little detail.

Nash spoke softly into her ear, "What about the cabin?"

Londyn shot him a quick smile and turned back to Julia. "No, thank you...and thank you for filling in for me until I could get here."

Julia waved a hand. "Oh, no problem. I know all the lines. I like to be prepared for anything."

"That's very convenient," Londyn said with a tight smile, keeping all sarcasm to herself. "I'll see you on the set." She turned with her bunch of dusty clothes clutched in her arms.

Nash placed a hand at the small of her back and walked with her toward the cabin. Once they were out of earshot, he said, "I'll have Swede do a background check on Julia."

Glad he was thinking along the same lines, she nodded. "Although I can't imagine where she'd get hold of C-4 or know how to set a detonator, it wouldn't hurt to know my potential competition." Londyn stopped in front of the cabin. "I'll only be a minute."

Nash touched her arm. "Let me check inside first."

Londyn didn't argue. He'd saved her from the explosion. Who knew what else might be lying in wait to surprise her?

Nash ducked into the cabin and was back out moments later. "All clear."

"Thanks." Londyn gave him a brief smile and ducked through the door. She shook the dust out of the clothes and laid them on the rough-hewn table built by the men who'd created their sets and props. She glanced at the uncovered windows. Morning sunlight shone across the wooden floor. Moving into the shadows, she stripped out of the T-shirt and baggy sweats Nash had loaned her. Then, she quickly pulled on the pants and white blouse the costume designer had provided for the scene. Immediately, she was enveloped in the potent floral scent Julia always wore.

The perfume tickled Londyn's nose and made her sneeze. She hoped it would fade before she had to say her lines. Already late for the shoot, she didn't want to have to do multiple takes should she start sneezing.

When she stepped out of the cabin, she found the hair stylist and makeup artist talking with Nash.

They were young and pretty and smiling up at the handsome man.

A stab of something hit Londyn square in the

chest, making her hands curl into fists and a flush of red fill her vision. It was anger, but not the kind of anger she was used to. Her eyes widened. Holy crap. Was she jealous?

She shook her head, trying to clear the emotion before the women turned toward her.

"Oh, good," the makeup artist said. She plopped a tall folding chair in front of Londyn. "We came prepared," she said. "Sit." The woman pulled a makeup palette from the satchel slung over her shoulder.

The hairstylist had her toolbelt strapped around her hips with hairbrushes, a flat iron and bottles of hairspray positioned around her. A long extension cord ran from the flat iron to somewhere around the corner of the cabin, probably hooked up to one of the site's generators.

Londyn dropped into the chair.

For the next few minutes, the women worked their magic on her makeup and hair. When they were done, they stepped back.

The makeup specialist tipped her head toward the set. "Go. They're waiting on you."

Londyn popped out of the chair and hurried to where the cameras were positioned. The cast and crew stood around, smoking, joking or generally looking bored.

Director Haynes stood with his arms crossed over

his chest, his toe tapping in the dust. When he spotted Londyn headed their way, he turned and shouted, "Let's get this ball rolling!"

People sprang into action. Cameramen ducked behind their cameras, and lighting technicians took their positions, adjusting the lighting. Troy and Craig stood in the middle of the set where they'd been when Londyn had first arrived.

Having read the script and witnessed the scene acted out with Julia playing her part, Londyn had a good idea of what was expected. Only she'd be damned if she dropped the gun.

"Remember, when you get the gun, you're to aim at Troy and pull the trigger," Haynes said. "The blank will sound just like a real bullet being discharged."

Having been raised by her grandfather, Londyn knew how to handle handguns, rifles, shotguns and even a flame thrower. Each had its purpose on the ranch. Her grandfather had made sure she could handle all of them and that she maintained her proficiency. He'd preached that when you needed a gun, you didn't have time to learn how to use it.

They'd spent many hours practicing with targets, aluminum cans, tree stumps and clay pigeons. He'd taken her hunting deer, elk, moose and pheasants. She'd bagged her limit on many occasions. Her grandfather had also taught her to fish. What they hadn't eaten immediately, they'd put in the freezer.

When money had been tight, they'd never lacked for meat.

Funny how images of her grandfather came up. He'd taught her so much about ranching, nature and responsibility. But this wasn't hunting and fishing. She was a fish out of water in the world of acting. If she wanted to save the ranch, she had to focus on getting her lines right and making her movements look natural. She didn't like having to shoot the same scene over and over. Her goal was to get it right the first time.

Nash stood behind the cameras while Londyn took her position.

As much as she liked her independence, not relying on anyone else, the feeling of being safe filled her heart and soul, making it easier to concentrate on the work she must do. She had to remind herself, *Don't get used to it.* Once the film was complete, she'd be back on her ranch, and Nash would go on to the next job. A sad feeling washed over her.

What did she expect? To Nash, she was *the job.* It wasn't like he'd fall in love with her and stay. And it wasn't like she'd fall in love with him. Watching her mother's three failed marriages, Londyn had decided long ago that marriage wasn't for her. Why tie yourself to a man when it never lasted? Falling in love wasn't worth the hassle and pain of divorce.

As Londyn prepared for the director to yell *Action!,* she glanced back at Nash with his broad shoulders, observant gaze and jagged scar along the side of his face. She could see where other women would find him attractive enough to fall in love with him. He was handsome, dedicated and concerned for her welfare. And his body had hers humming with the simplest of touches. And his kiss...

Her pulse ratcheted up, and her cheeks filled with heat. Now was not the time to remember that kiss.

Focus, girl! He's your bodyguard, nothing more.

Then why did he feel like so much more?

NASH STOOD BACK, wishing he could be closer to Londyn. The distance between them wasn't great, but it was enough to make him edgy.

What if Troy was too rough on her? What if the gun he pointed at her head suddenly went off? Sure, they were using blanks, but a blank fired at close range could kill someone. With the barrel of the pistol pressed against her temple, all it would take was for Troy to get careless and squeeze the trigger.

The rush of dread sent Nash stepping forward.

"Action!" Haynes yelled.

Troy grabbed Londyn and pressed the handgun to her temple.

Nash held his breath, willing Londyn to fake-fight her way out of Troy's hold quickly before the man got stupid and pulled the trigger.

He didn't have long to wait until Londyn jabbed

her elbow into the man's gut, grabbed his hand and twisted his arm around, divesting him of the weapon.

She shoved the man away from her and aimed the handgun at him. "Stay back, or I'll shoot," she called out.

Troy hesitated for only a moment, then lunged toward her.

Londyn aimed the gun at Troy. A moment later, she pulled the trigger.

A loud bang sounded, followed almost instantly by the crashing sound of one of the lighting fixtures.

"Cut! Cut!" Haynes yelled. "What the hell was that?"

Nash rushed forward and hovered over Londyn, using his body as a shield. "Are you okay?" he asked.

Londyn stared down at the gun she'd taken from Troy and looked past Troy to the lighting fixture that had been destroyed.

"Oh my God," Londyn said. "That was a live round."

"Holy shit." Troy's eyes rounded as he ran his hands over his chest.

Londyn shook her head. "Don't worry," she said. "I didn't shoot at you, but over your shoulder."

Troy's face blanched. "What if you hadn't missed?"

Londyn shook her head. "Did you hear me? I wasn't aiming at you. I didn't miss. I never aim at anything I don't want to kill," she said. "Although I didn't really want to kill the light, it was what I aimed for. If I'd aimed at you, I wouldn't have missed." She turned to Haynes.

Haynes scrubbed a hand down his face. "JP!"

The props man rushed into the center of the set. "Give me the gun."

Londyn handed over the pistol.

"I put blanks in this weapon," JP said. "The magazine was empty when I started. I very carefully checked the box I took the blanks from and placed them in the magazine one at a time. I know I was right. I even put a mark on the magazine when I finished." He expelled the magazine from the weapon, dropping it into his hand. "See? I put my initials on the side of the—"

Nash studied the magazine, as JP turned it over several times. He didn't see any marks on the metal casing.

JP looked up, his gaze meeting Director Haynes's. "It's not there. My mark is not on this magazine. This is not the magazine I placed in the gun." He turned the weapon over to the side with the serial number. "This is the gun, but not the magazine I loaded specifically with blanks. Someone switched magazines."

Londyn's face lost some of its color beneath her dark complexion. She leaned into Nash. "I could've killed a man," she said softly.

Nash slipped an arm around her waist and pulled her close. "But you didn't," he reminded her.

"Steve told me to aim at Troy." She shook her head. "I couldn't. My grandfather instilled years of training in me. Only aim a loaded weapon at something if you plan to kill it." She looked up into Nash's eyes. "I couldn't aim at Troy like I was told. I shifted my aim to an inanimate object."

Nash smoothed a strand of her hair back off her cheek. "The lights."

"God dammit," Steve Haynes blasted. He turned slowly in a three-hundred-sixty-five-degree circle, his eyes narrowed, his cheeks a ruddy red. "Who the hell switched the magazines?"

When no one answered, the director shook his head. "Someone on this set is fucking with us. When I find out who...so help me, I'll..." He slammed his fist into his palm.

"You'll turn him over to the law," Londyn said. "For attempted murder." She lifted her head. "This incident needs to be reported to the sheriff."

"Thankfully, no one was injured," Haynes said. "But we're down one light now. It'll take time to get another shipped out to this godforsaken location."

"I'll get right on it," a man called out.

"Someone call the sheriff," Haynes said. "The sooner he gets out here, the sooner we can get back to work. At this rate, we won't finish shooting before the first snow."

A man walked up to the director and spoke softly

to him, but loud enough, Nash could hear what he said.

"I can't do this," the cameraman said. "I have a wife and two kids at home. I'm their only source of income. If I'm shot or taken out in an explosion, they're screwed. I'm sorry, but I'm going home before something happens to me."

"Marty, you can't quit now," Haynes said. "We need you."

The man shook his head. "My family needs me more. Some of the guys think this project is cursed. At first, I didn't believe them. But now..."

"It's not cursed," Haynes said. "But if that's how you feel... You have to do what you think is best. However, you'll have to wait until the sheriff has a chance to talk to everyone. In the meantime, pack your gear."

The man nodded and left the set.

Haynes's gaze followed the man until he disappeared. Then he turned toward the rest of the cast and crew. "Anyone else believe this project is cursed and want to leave now?"

A man stepped forward. "I've got a new baby at home. I want to be around to watch her grow."

"Fine," Haynes said. "Pack your things. You can leave when the sheriff says you can go."

The man left the gathering.

Haynes stood taller, holding his head high. "I don't believe in cursed projects, bad juju or whatever bullshit you want to call it. There is nothing magical or mystical about being targeted by some sadistic bastard."

Nash agreed. This wasn't the ghosts of Native American ancestors trying to scare them off sacred grounds. A living man or men was behind the incidents.

"What concerns me most," Haynes said, "is that whoever is doing this has to be someone among us." He stared around at the people gathered. "We *will* find out who is responsible. When we do, I'll do everything in my power to put him in jail. If that's not enough, I'll get him blackballed, so he'll never again work in the movie industry. For those of you who decide to stay for the duration of this project, I advise you all to watch your backs. Now, while we're waiting for the sheriff, let's continue with this scene from the point where we left off. JP, get Lana another gun, preferably one that isn't loaded. Bag this one. I'm sure the sheriff will confiscate it for evidence."

Nash lowered his mouth close to Londyn's ear. "Are you okay?"

She nodded. "I am."

"Up to continuing?" Nash persisted.

"Yes," she sighed. "We don't know if the sheriff will shut us down when he hears about this latest attempt. I'm sure Haynes wants to get more done before that might happen."

JP appeared beside Londyn, carrying a small gun

case. He flipped it open and extracted a handgun much like the one that had had the real bullets in it. He pulled back the bolt and showed Nash and Londyn that the chamber was empty. Then he dropped the magazine from the handle and let Londyn inspect it to see that it, too, was empty.

Then he slipped the empty magazine into the handle and handed the weapon to Londyn. He left the set with the empty case and the gun containing the real bullets.

Nash didn't envy the guy. He'd have to explain to the sheriff how he'd managed the gun up to the point it had ended up in Londyn's hands with real bullets, not blanks.

"Everyone in position," Haynes called out.

Cast and crew hurried to take their places.

Londyn's hand shook slightly as she stood in front of Troy, holding the gun.

Nash hated backing away behind the cameras. He could only guess at what might happen next. Whoever was behind all the attacks was employing different methods to target Londyn or set her up on murder charges.

As Londyn performed her part, Nash texted Swede, letting him know what had happened and urging him to send any background information he could find on the cast and crew. Whoever it was causing the problems understood explosives and guns. If he had any kind of criminal record, it should show up.

And if the guy had never been charged with a crime?

They were screwed until they caught him in the act.

Swede let him know Hank and Sadie were on their way and told him to expect them within the hour.

CHAPTER 7

Londyn made it through the scene, not entirely happy with her performance.

By the look on Hayne's face, he wasn't happy either. "Again!" he yelled.

Everyone resumed their positions from the start of the sequence.

"Action!" Haynes called out.

No sooner had the action started than a thumping sound thrummed in the air.

Haynes glanced toward the sky. "Cut!"

A helicopter roared into view, hovered over a nearby field and slowly descended.

Haynes groaned. "What now?"

Once the helicopter touched down, the side door slid open, and a man dropped to the ground. He turned and reached for the small woman standing in the door. Grabbing her around her waist, he swung her out of the aircraft and into his arms as if she weighed nothing.

She laughed, wrapped her arms around his neck and kissed him. Then she tapped her palms against his chest.

The man lowered the woman to her feet. She stood a good head shorter than the man and had bright golden-blond hair.

The man reached into the chopper, retrieved a large duffel bag and slung it over his shoulder. The blonde took the man's hand and hurried toward the cast and crew poised to shoot the next scene.

"Holy shit," Craig Ryland murmured. "That's Sadie McClain."

Word spread fast as the actors and crew abandoned their positions to greet the famous actress.

"Oh, please," Sadie waved toward the cameras, "don't let us halt progress. We'll be quiet."

Haynes shook his head and moved to intercept the woman who was considered Hollywood royalty.

"Ms. McClain," he said. "It's an honor to have you on our set. To what do we owe the pleasure?"

Sadie graced the man with her million-dollar smile. "We came to see Miss Tyler-Lovejoy. But if she's in the middle of a scene, we can wait until you can take a break."

"If you don't mind," Haynes said. "We're on a tight schedule and have a bigger scene we want to get to before the storms reach us."

"By all means." Sadie waved toward the set. "Carry on."

Hank and Sadie stood silently with Nash while Londyn, Craig and Troy went through the scene again.

Having a mega-star watching made Londyn even more nervous than she'd been when they'd shot her very first scene. Thankfully, her nerves helped make her desperate fight to be free of Troy look even more convincing. As well, she'd practiced her lines enough, she said them without error.

When Haynes yelled, "Cut!" Londyn felt drained. Being "on" all the time took a lot out of her. The introvert inside her wasn't used to being with so many people watching her every move. She much preferred a herd of cattle over people any day.

As the director reviewed the footage, Londyn remained on the set, holding her breath. Some scenes were repeated five or six times. They didn't have time for that many takes if they hoped to film the cattle drive that afternoon.

"It'll do," Haynes announced.

Londyn grinned at the collective sigh from cast and crew, only for her smile to fade when the sheriff pulled into the parking area.

For the next couple of hours, every person ran the gauntlet of questions. Haynes had those who weren't being questioned working to prepare the equipment they would need to film the cattle drive.

Londyn hurried toward Nash and the two people with him. A crowd had gathered around them, gushing over Sadie McClain.

As Londyn neared, Hank held up his hand. "If you all don't mind, we came to see Miss Tyler-Lovejoy."

The crowd around Sadie slowly dispersed, leaving Londyn, Nash, Hank and Sadie alone.

Nash touched Londyn's arm. "Are you okay?"

Londyn nodded, liking the reassuring feel of his hand on her arm as if it grounded her. "I'm fine."

"You look pale," he said, his frown deepening.

"I'm just tired." She nodded toward Hank and Sadie. "Are you going to introduce me?"

"Yes, of course." Nash turned to the movie star. "Londyn Tyler-Lovejoy, this is Sadie McClain."

Sadie smiled and held out her hand. "Hank tells me this is your first ever movie." She shook her head. "You were amazing in that scene. I was absolutely convinced by your performance."

"You're too kind."

"No, really. I don't say that to just anyone. If you don't have any movie experience, you must have done theater."

Londyn shook her head. "None. Not even in high school."

"No?" Sadie's blue eyes widened. "Your mother is Dana Tyler, right?"

"Yes, ma'am," Londyn responded, still holding Sadie's hand.

"She didn't get you into acting at an early age?"

"No, ma'am. My grandfather raised me on our ranch in Montana, far away from Hollywood."

Sadie sighed. "Then it must be hereditary. She's a very talented actor. I've followed her career for years and hope to be half as good as she is at this profession."

Londyn's brow twisted. "You're already at the top of your career. You're one of the most sought-after talents in the industry."

"But I can always learn more," Sadie insisted. "Especially from someone like Dana Tyler." She patted their joined hands with her free one and let go. "But here I am fangirling, and you haven't met the man who keeps me sane. Londyn, this is my husband, Hank Patterson."

Hank Patterson was every bit as big, muscular and broad-chested as Nash. He engulfed her hand in his and gripped it firmly. "Miss Tyler-Lovejoy, it's a pleasure to meet you. Your mother had good things to say about you. After seeing you act in that scene, I can see why she's so proud."

Londyn snorted softly. "The only acting she's seen me do was when she prepared me for the audition. I can only hope to be half the actor she is."

"From what we saw, I'd say you're well on your way to meeting your goal." Hank nodded toward Nash. "Swede has kept me up to date on what happened yesterday and what law enforcement is doing to find the person responsible for the explosion."

Sadie pressed a hand to her heart. "I'm so sorry about your trailer, but I'm glad you weren't in it."

"Thanks," Londyn said.

Hank continued, "Nash briefed me on the live bullets in the prop gun." He shook his head. "Good for you not aiming for the other actor. That scene could've ended a whole lot worse." He released her hand. "We stopped at your ranch on the way down from Eagle Rock. Sadie collected everything on your list while I touched bases with your ranch hands and your neighbor, Ben Standing Bear."

Londyn leaned toward Hank, eager for news. "How is everything back home? I haven't called in the past few days with everything that's happened. Did they get the hay cut? Did the farrier make it out to work with the horses? Did they get the fence mended on the south pasture?"

Hank chuckled. "Let's see if I can remember what Ben told me. Yes, the hay was cut, baled and stored in the barn. Yes, the farrier came. No problems. The south fence was mended, a tree fell on the west fence and a couple of steers found their way onto Ben's place. His people rounded them up and moved them back onto your spread. Your paint mare had a filly. Mare and filly are doing great. Tom, the barn cat, had five kittens. And so far, everything is running smoothly."

"Tom's a female? He's very skittish but a great mouser. Or should I say she?" Londyn shook her head. "I can't believe Tom had kittens. And I'm glad the mare had a filly. Did she have her dam's markings?"

Hank nodded. "She's a beauty like her mother."

Sadie laughed. "I had to remind Hank we needed to get your care package to Yellowstone, or he would've gone on a tour of the ranch with Ben and your ranch hands."

Tears welled in Londyn's eyes. "Thank you for the update." A single tear escaped and ran down her cheek. She brushed it away and tried to laugh. "Sorry. I didn't realize just how much I missed home."

Sadie touched her arm. "I know how you feel. When I left Montana to pursue my acting career, I think I cried for a month. I never stopped missing home." She slipped her hand through the crook of Hank's elbow. "Now, I get to be home as often as possible with my husband and children."

"In between movie contracts," Hank amended. "Sometimes we bring a little bit of home to her on location."

Sadie smiled. "That's right. Hank came with me to Jordan recently. His team provided security for the production company. It was nice having him there," her smile slipped, "though I missed our babies. I don't like being away from them for long. I never go more than two weeks without seeing them. I've gotten to where I'm not signing up for as many projects as I did BK."

"BK?" Londyn asked.

Hank chuckled. "Before kids."

Londyn liked Hank and Sadie. For a movie star and the hotshot founder of what seemed like the fastest-growing security company in the US, the pair were down to earth, loving and seemed to really care about others. Even complete strangers like Londyn.

"Speaking of kids..." Sadie glanced up at her husband.

Hank nodded and turned to Nash. "You know, all you have to do is call or text, and we can send backup. I can have them here in less than two hours, especially since we have a helicopter now."

"Thanks," Nash said. "I'll keep that in mind."

Hank glanced around at the people scurrying about, moving equipment. "I'd love to stay and watch the cattle drive, but as my wife reminds me, we need to get back to the kids."

Sadie grimaced. "Not that they'll miss us as much as we miss them. Uncle Chuck and Aunt Kate are staying with them right now, and they brought their little boy Oliver with them. I'm not sure how much the adults can stand with a couple of hell-raising four-year-olds. Emma tries to keep them in line, but those two boys together seem to find trouble."

"Right." Hank shook Nash's hand. "We'd better get back before they burn the house down." He waved toward the vehicles parked nearby. "I can stash your things in Nash's truck. If you need anything else, let us know. It might be a day or two before we can make the trip back down."

"I'm sure I'll be fine," Londyn said. "Thank you for going out of your way to pick up my things. And thank you for bringing news from home. I'll be glad when this project wraps up." She shook her head. "I don't know how you do this for a living."

Sadie shrugged. "It paid the bills. Now, I only take projects I truly love. I'd much rather be home with my family. Come see us when you can. We'd love to have you and Nash stay at White Oak Ranch with us."

Hank and Sadie set off across the field and climbed into the helicopter. Moments later, the rotors started spinning, and the aircraft lifted off the ground and banked toward the northwest.

"That was really nice of them to go to all the trouble of going to my ranch for my things. It'll be nice to have clothes that fit. Not that I didn't appreciate your contribution to my modesty." Londyn said with a twisted grin. Her gaze followed the chopper until it disappeared. She turned to Nash. "Hungry?"

"I am," he said. "What do you do for food when you're in a remote location? I can't imagine everyone drives into town to the nearest fast-food restaurant."

Londyn snorted. "Considering the nearest restaurant is thirty minutes or more away, they bring food to us. We've had a chuckwagon preparing pretty decent meals. Since we're tight on time, I don't know what they'll have, but let's find out. I'm starving."

Londyn found people gathered around the chuck wagon where the cook had hamburgers and hotdogs sizzling on the grill.

Londyn grabbed a paper plate and a bun and held it out for the cook to deposit a charred hamburger patty in the middle. She went back to the table with all the fixings and loaded her burger with lettuce, tomatoes and dill pickles. A squirt of mustard, a handful of potato chips, and she was set.

Nash appeared beside her with two burger patties on his bun and a dollop of mustard.

She cocked an eyebrow. "What? No vegetables?"

"This is easier," he said.

"Not even a pickle?" she asked.

He shook his head. "When I'm feeling particularly civilized, I might opt for a pickle. But this is enough."

After the gravity of the explosion the day before and the horror of nearly killing one of her castmates, Londyn relaxed in their light-hearted teasing about their inconsequential preferences of toppings on a burger.

Taking it a step further, she said, "I can understand no lettuce or tomato. And, yes, I skip the onion when I don't want to blast anyone with onion breath." Londyn shook her head. "But a hamburger isn't a hamburger without a dill pickle. That's pretty much a dealbreaker. I could never be with someone who doesn't put a pickle on his burger."

Nash tossed a handful of potato chips onto his plate, then turned to follow her to a picnic table. "You set a high bar for a woman who showed up for work this morning in baggy sweatpants."

Londyn swallowed the giggle that threatened to bubble up her throat. She laid her plate on the table and sat on the bench. "You have a point. But a girl's gotta draw the line somewhere."

"Yes, she does." Nash laid his plate beside hers rather than across the table and slid onto the bench.

His thigh bumped against hers, setting off an electrical charge that shot through her system like a lightning bolt and got her blood pumping hard through her veins. She sucked in a breath, held it and let it out slowly, willing her pulse to return to normal.

Nash held up a package. "You might reconsider when you realize I snagged the last package of chocolate chip cookies."

Londyn tipped her head. "You think I'd lower my standards for a cookie?"

"A chocolate chip cookie." He waved the package under her nose.

"Mr. Nelson, as much as I hate to admit it..." Londyn heaved an exaggerated sigh, "you're absolutely correct. I can be swayed. But not for anything less than a chocolate chip cookie."

"Let's be clear...I don't have to put a pickle on my burger to be with you?"

She shook her head. "Not if you come bearing gifts involving chocolate chips."

He tore open the package, extracted a cookie and held it out. "And they said she couldn't be bought."

"In a heartbeat." She plucked the cookie from his hand and sank her teeth into it.

Nash's eyes narrowed, the corners of his lips twitching as if he were holding back a smile. "Aren't you supposed to finish your meal before you jump right into dessert?"

"I'm a firm believer in having dessert first," Londyn said as she chewed.

Nash grinned. "Obviously."

"Given the attempts on my life," Londyn said, "I might not make it to dessert."

Nash's grin disappeared. He reached for her hand and held it in his. "I'm going to do everything in my power to see that you make it to dessert."

She stared down at the hand holding hers. It was such a simple touch, yet it was like dropping a lit torch into a huge box of fireworks.

Her heart raced, her pulse pounded so loudly in her ears as to be deafening and every nerve exploded, sending a cacophony of messages zinging to her brain.

"You have my promise," he added. Then he

removed his hand from hers and lifted his pickle-less burger to his lips.

Londyn sat for a few moments longer, her brain trying to process the assault on her senses.

Was she so starved for affection that all a man had to do was hold her hand, and she'd forget her name or how to breathe?

No.

Not any man.

Hank had held her hand in his, and nothing had happened to make her lose her mind.

Nash was the only man who'd ever set her body and her world spinning out of control with a simple touch.

And frankly, it scared the shit out of her.

CHAPTER 8

Nash ate the burger, although he didn't really taste it. When Londyn had joked about not making it to dessert, her words had hit too close to home.

They'd been teasing about the criteria a man had to meet to be with Londyn. He'd insisted all he needed on a burger was meat and a bun. But it was more than that.

Her insistence on pickles made him want to go back to the table with the pickles and pour the entire container onto his damned, meat-only burger. Only then would he prove he could rise to her bar, and they could be together, according to her standard.

But could they?

He shoved the last of his burger into his mouth, chewed and swallowed the evidence that could eliminate him as a potential candidate for Miss Tyler-Lovejoy's interest.

It didn't matter that his hamburger preference was different than hers. What did matter was that he was only the employee—there to protect the movie star client.

He hadn't counted on the movie star being so...exotically beautiful, independent and courageous.

She was nothing like what he'd expected. He'd built up in his mind a spoiled actress, imagining sabotaged props to get attention from her celebrity mother. He'd thought this was more a job of babysitting a spoiled little rich girl with nothing more dangerous than fans invading her personal space.

What he'd found was a woman uncomfortable with her role as a performer. A girl more comfortable on a ranch in Montana than among the glitz and glamor of Hollywood's elite.

A woman whose touch ignited a fire at his very core he hadn't felt in...well, forever. No woman had made him feel the way he did when he was with Londyn.

And the danger had escalated exponentially within the first few minutes on the job. An explosion, no less. The very thing that threw him back to his last mission in Afghanistan. The one that had left him wounded in body and spirit.

After months of therapy for his injury and for PTSD, he'd thought he was ready to face the world and the job.

Now...he wasn't so sure.

A few of his panic attacks had left him almost catatonic. What good would he be to Londyn if he froze in the heat of battle?

He'd just promised to see her through to dessert. Which, to him, meant he'd promised to keep her alive.

Could he live up to that promise? Or should he call Hank now and tell him to send a replacement?

He wasn't ready.

The thought of someone else taking over and providing for Londyn's protection made Nash's gut bunch into a knot.

If Hank pulled him off the job and sent him back to West Yellowstone to pick up some security detail for a sporting event or rodeo, would he be able to quit thinking about Londyn? Would he stop worrying about her?

He gave himself a moment to think about it.

No.

He wouldn't stop worrying about her, wondering if whoever was after her had gotten past her protector and finished the job the explosion had not.

It scared him more than anything he'd ever encountered in special operations warfare.

He shot a glance toward Londyn.

She nibbled on her burger, her eyes on her plate, not him.

What was she thinking?

Had he come on too strong with his promise to

keep her safe? Had holding her hand made her uncomfortable?

His breathing became more labored, and his heart pounded against his ribs. If it got any faster, he'd be in a full-on panic attack. The last thing Londyn needed was for her hired bodyguard to freak out.

Using some of the techniques his therapist had taught him, he focused on breathing, forcing air in and out of his lungs in long, slow breaths. He willed his pulse to slow, his heart to relax and his thoughts to still.

Londyn's hand covered his on the tabletop, sending his heart into orbit again, his pulse racing, pounding so loud in his ears he could hear little else.

"Hey," she said. "Are you all right?"

"I am." He turned his hand over and gripped hers. He prayed she didn't feel the vibrations of his hand shaking.

"I know you're going to do everything you can to protect me," she started, "but I want you to know that if all else fails and I die, please let Ben Standing Bear know. He'll break the news to my ranch hands. I guess my mother will ultimately inherit the ranch should I not survive. She has a lawyer who will help her sell the ranch."

"You think she'll sell it?"

Londyn nodded. "I know she will. She never wanted to come back. Not even to see me. I'd have to fly out to Hollywood when she wanted time with me."

"Did you resent her for that?"

"No," Londyn said. "She could've forced me to live in California with her. But after one summer on the ranch, I knew where I wanted to be. She didn't like that she couldn't see me whenever she wanted or had time to, but I didn't like Hollywood."

"So, she just let your grandfather raise you?"

Londyn nodded. "Yes. I was six years old when I came to stay with my grandfather for the summer. I told my mother that I never wanted to leave. That if she loved me, she'd let me stay with him."

"A little emotional blackmail?" Nash suggested.

"Is it blackmail if you ask for what they want anyway?" Londyn challenged.

"Was it what your mother wanted?" Nash asked.

"I believed it was," Londyn said. "The bonus was that I would be with family—my grandfather— instead of a nanny. I'd gotten quite a few nannies fired in my short life. I was done with them. Meanwhile, my mother was busy getting her career off the ground. Having a small child held her back. It wasn't until I went to live with my grandfather that her career took off." She raised her hands, palms up. "I was in her way. What else would I think?"

"Your mother seems to care now," Nash said.

"Or she wants to take credit for finding the right person for the part...?" Londyn drew in a deep breath and let it out slowly. "Whatever it was, I took this job to save the ranch without having to rely on my mother's wealth to bail me out."

"Wasn't taking this job allowing your mother to bail you out?" Nash asked softly.

Londyn's jaw hardened, and her eyes narrowed. "She might have gotten me the audition, but I'm the one who has to perform. I'm working for the money they're paying. I will not take handouts."

A sheriff's deputy approached. "We're ready to interview you, Miss Tyler-Lovejoy."

Londyn rose from the picnic table and gathered her paper plate and half-eaten hamburger with the pickle. "Let me discard my trash, and I'm all yours."

Nash's gaze followed her, knowing how much she hated the interruptions. But she hated even worse what could have happened.

Her decision to aim at something rather than someone had spared Troy's life.

Anyone else would have followed the director's instructions, aimed at Troy, and Troy would have been injured or killed.

But Londyn wasn't anyone else. She'd been raised on a ranch by her grandfather. The man had taught her well about the proper use of deadly weapons.

Yeah, Londyn Tyler-Lovejoy was nothing like what Nash had imagined.

She was so much more.

. . .

BY THE TIME the sheriff and his deputy left, the cast and crew were ready to move on to where the cattle drive scene would take place.

Haynes had contracted with a local rancher to use his herd and horses.

Londyn was ready to get it over with. Being questioned by the sheriff two days in a row, performing physically and emotionally draining scenes for the movie and coming to grips with the attraction she was feeling for her bodyguard were taking its toll.

The crew went ahead of the cast to a ranch adjacent to Yellowstone National Park. Londyn changed into the costume provided for the cattle drive scene, wanting to hit the ground running as soon as the director called for action.

She'd spoken with Haynes about allowing Nash to be one of the cowboys on the cattle drive. The costume designer scrambled to find something that would fit Nash's broad shoulders. Fortunately, he'd come with his own cowboy hat, which he'd left in his truck.

He wouldn't let Londyn close to her truck or trailer until he had performed a thorough inspection, searching for explosives, checking the brakes and looking over the engine for any sign of tampering. When he was done, he helped her load her horse into the trailer.

Londyn closed the trailer door and secured the latch. She faced Nash and lifted her chin. "I'll drive."

"Are you sure?" His gaze held hers. "I'm experienced driving trucks with livestock trailers."

Her eyes narrowed. "I know, but I need to be in control of this one thing. Especially since everything else in my life seems to be spinning completely out of my control."

"Okay," he said.

She'd expected him to argue. His short response took the starch out of her.

"I have no problem riding shotgun," he added. "It leaves me free to shoot if the need arises." He made no move to get into the truck. Instead, he took another step toward her, raised his hand and cupped her cheek. "Either way, I'll be with you all the way." Then he dipped his head, and his mouth connected with hers. He broke away, spun on his booted heels and strode to the driver's door of the truck. He pulled it open and held it for her.

Londyn raised her fingers to her lips. They still tingled from the light brush with his. His simple touch left her brain scrambled and set her pulse into high gear. As she walked toward him, she had the wildest urge to take that kiss to the next level. Rather than climbing into the driver's seat, she stopped in front of him and stared up into his eyes. "Why did you do that?"

"Do what?"

"Kiss me," she said softly.

"Two reasons. One, it seemed like the right thing to do at the time. Two, it was the only thing I could control." His lips twisted, and he shook his head. "Except it backfired."

Londyn frowned. "How so?"

He gave her a weak smile. "Now, I don't even have control over my response to that kiss. All I want to do is kiss you again. Please, get in the truck before my lack of control results in yet another kiss."

Londyn's breath hitched in her chest. Every muscle, every nerve and every inclination urged her to follow through with her initial instinct. She leaned up on her toes, wrapped her hand behind the back of his neck and pulled his face closer. When her lips met his, she felt a shocking combination of raw desire and the feeling of having come home.

NASH SAT in the passenger seat on the drive over to the ranch where the cattle drive would be filmed. He remained on high alert, aware of his surroundings at all times. More disturbing, he was aware of Londyn in the seat beside him. The scent of her shampoo wafted in the air. The feel of her lips against his lingered in his senses. How—in two days—could one woman get under his skin so completely?

Maybe the act of brushing her hair the night before was where it began. Unlike brushing his little sisters' hair, working the tangles out of Londyn's had been anything but brotherly. Her thick black hair, as much a part of her heritage as her high cheekbones and richly toned skin, had him thinking about how her black hair would look spread across a white pillowcase or cascading over her naked shoulders.

He'd had a major boner by the time he'd finished. Just thinking about running his hands through her hair had his groin tightening all over again.

He stared at the wide-open expanse of prairie land stretched before them. Places like this brought a calm he hadn't felt in a long time. He could get used to this.

"What made you decide to join the Army?" Londyn asked, breaking the silence stretching between them.

"My stepfather. I had a huge amount of respect for the man. He deployed often, but when he came home, he didn't try to take over from my mother. He shared the household chores, setting an example for us kids. He was strong and proud of his country and his contribution to protecting it and his family. I wanted to be like him."

"He sounds amazing." She stared at the road ahead. "I never knew my father. Thankfully, Gramps filled that hole in my life." She sighed. "I grew up wanting to be like him. I miss him."

"The thing about losing someone you care about is that you don't ever lose them completely," Nash said. "They're always with you in your heart and in your memories."

Londyn glanced his way, a frown denting her forehead. "Do you still have your parents?"

Nash grinned. "I do. Now that they're empty-nesters, they sold their house, bought a motorhome and travel the country."

"Where are they now?" Londyn asked.

Nash tilted his head, his eyes narrowing. "I think they were headed for the Upper Peninsula of Michigan this week. They're making their way through all the national parks, concentrating on the ones up north during the summer, then moving south for the winter."

"And your sisters? Where are they now?"

"Maddie lives in Seattle, working for a high-tech firm. She and her fiancé are getting married in December. They wanted a winter wedding in Whistler, Canada. Juju." Nash chuckled. "Juliet. She hates being called Juju. She lives in San Diego with her Navy SEAL husband and has her own travel agency. She's been all over the world, and she's only twenty-seven."

"What about sister number three?"

"Mona and I were the most alike. We were both into sports, and both of us wanted to follow in our father's footsteps. I enlisted as soon as I graduated high school. She was always the smarter one. She went to college, joined ROTC and entered the Army as a Second Lieutenant. Where I learned how to jump out of helicopters and airplanes, she learned how to fly them. She kicks ass as a pilot."

"You're very proud of your family," Londyn noted.

He smiled. "Damn right, I am."

"As much as you love your family, I'm surprised you don't have a family of your own." She shot a glance his way. "At least, I assume you don't."

His lips twisted. "I don't."

"Why not?" she asked. "You can tell me to mind my own business. It won't hurt my feelings. It's really none of my business."

"It's okay," he said. "I married a woman I met in Basic Combat Training. We were young, stupid and didn't know what we were doing. Since neither one of us had much rank, the Army didn't make it a priority to station us together. We spent the first two years of our married life apart. When I was deployed to the Middle East, she met a man who wasn't in the military. She asked for a divorce."

"I'm sorry."

"I'm not. We weren't ready for commitment. We were so young we ended up outgrowing each other." He shrugged. "We still stay in touch. She got out of the Army, had four kids and is happily teaching fifth-graders."

Londyn laughed. "Is anyone happy teaching fifth-graders? I know I was a handful then, as was every other kid in my class. So, she found her soul mate.

You didn't?"

Nash shook his head. "I wasn't looking. When you're in Special Forces, you never know when you're going to deploy. You spend very little time at home. It's not conducive to long-term relationships."

"I guess not." Londyn slowed, turned onto a gravel road and passed through a gate, bumping over the metal grate of a cattleguard. "Did you retire from the military?"

Nash looked at the dusty road ahead. "Medically retired, as are many of the people Hank hires. Not good enough for active duty, but we still have a lot of life left in us."

Londyn tilted her. "You seem physically fit."

Nash gritted his teeth. "Not by Army standards. Tell me what the premise of the movie you're making is. I've only seen two scenes, and I have no idea."

"It's about a young Native American woman who inherits a ranch from a white man who raised her after her parents died in an automobile accident he was responsible for."

"Sounds familiar," he said, giving her a pointed look.

She nodded. "There are some similarities that make the part easy for me to portray. The difference is that my parents aren't dead. At least my mother isn't dead. I have no idea who my father is. And the man who raised me was truly my grandfather."

"Okay, but you did inherit your ranch from the

man who raised you." He cocked an eyebrow. "I would think inheriting a ranch is a gift that would make the person happy. So, what is the conflict?"

"Besides missing the man she'd come to think of as a father figure, she owns a ranch. She's a female in a male-dominated world. And she's Shoshone in an area where many white men are highly prejudiced against Native Americans. It's a story of her struggles to prove herself when others want her to fail."

Nash frowned. "Have you run into situations like that, having inherited your ranch?"

She shrugged. "No one has been blatantly angry or ugly to me. However, I don't get the same respect or treatment when I take my cattle to auction or purchase feed at the feed store. Men tend to think I'm not capable of managing a ranch. What they don't know is that my grandfather taught me everything he knew about running the ranch, raising cattle and managing the land. I can ride as well or better than any man in the state of Montana. I've helped countless cows deliver breech calves, trained my own horse, and cut, baled and hauled hay. I've branded, culled and castrated steers. And yet, my male counterparts who don't know me ask to talk to my husband or father when they want to discuss business."

"And the character you portray?"

"Gets the same treatment and worse. The villain is angered by the fact she's a female and Native

American. He feels she doesn't deserve the ranch and has no business owning or operating it in a white man's world. He wants her to disappear and is intent on making it happen."

"Do you think whoever is targeting you has the same issues with your inheritance?" Nash asked.

She shook her head. "I was doing just fine on my ranch with the help of my neighbor. There were no 'accidents' or attempts on my life. It wasn't until I landed this role and came to work in Wyoming on the movie set that things started happening."

"Could it be that your time on the film location is an opportunity for someone to sabotage your efforts without casting suspicion on himself back home?" Nash asked. "Someone who wants you to lose your ranch and maybe gain from your loss?"

Her brow knitted. "I can't imagine who would gain from me losing my ranch."

Nash tapped his fingers on the knee. "Has anyone approached you in an attempt to buy your property?"

"No."

"If you lose the property because you owe back taxes, couldn't someone pay those back taxes and take ownership of that property?"

"Maybe. But I'd think the bank that carries the mortgage would foreclose on it and try to sell it before the government could confiscate it for the back taxes."

"Have any of your neighbors ever expressed an

interest in buying the property?" Nash's eyes narrowed. "It would make sense if one of them wants to expand their own holdings."

"Our neighbors have always been there to help when we needed it, and we've reciprocated. I can't imagine any of them trying to kill me in hopes of taking the ranch." She flung her hand in the air. "I don't know. I've always felt like we were all just trying to survive and had each other's backs."

"Greed can change—"

The truck swayed suddenly.

Londyn gripped the steering wheel with both hands.

"What was that?" Nash asked.

"Something's happening with the trailer. It's tugging on the truck's hitch." Londyn took her foot off the accelerator, her gaze going to the rearview mirror.

The truck jerked again.

"This isn't right." Londyn brought the truck to a stop, shifted into park and pushed open her door.

A loud bang sounded from the trailer, and it rocked on its wheels.

"It's Butterscotch," Londyn said and ran to the rear of the trailer.

The mare let out a startling scream that curdled Nash's blood. The trailer shook violently as the animal inside slammed its hooves against the inside walls.

Londyn unhooked the latch.

"Wait," Nash said. "She's upset. You open that door, and there's no telling what she'll do."

Londyn hesitated.

Butterscotch kicked the walls again and screamed like nothing Nash had ever heard before.

"At the rate she'd going, if I don't open the door and bring her out, she'll kill herself." Londyn yanked open the heavy metal door.

Nash grabbed Londyn and pulled her back behind the door as Butterscotch leaped through for the opening.

Her lead stopped her at first.

Her eyes were wide, and she was foaming at the mouth, lunging and fighting against her tether.

The metal loop on the trailer wall where her rope was attached snapped.

The buckskin leaped out the door.

"Butterscotch!" Londyn pushed free of Nash and dove for the lead.

The mare reared, her hooves coming so close to Londyn.

Nash's heart leaped into his throat. He grabbed her around her waist and hauled her back against him.

The mare came down on all fours and took off like her tail was on fire, bucking and kicking as she raced across the prairie.

"No!" Londyn fought her way free of Nash's rip.

"Butterscotch!" She ran after the horse.

Nash followed. Though pain shot through his knee, he kept going, cursing the injury that had ended his Army career. He didn't catch up with Londyn until she'd gone nearly a hundred yards.

By then, the mare had disappeared into a dusty haze.

Londyn slowed to a stop, breathing hard. She bent at the waist and braced her hands on her knees. "Have to...find her." She shook her head. "She's never... run free. She won't...survive...on... her own."

She dragged in a ragged breath and started running again.

Nash didn't let her get too far this time. Reaching out to grab her arm, he pulled her to a stop.

"Let go of me," she cried, tears running down her cheeks. "I...have to...find her."

Nash pulled her into his arms and held her. "We will. But we can't do it on foot. We'll need help."

"She doesn't know...how to survive...in the wild." Londyn buried her face against his chest. "She'll die."

"No. She won't," Nash insisted. "We'll find her."

Her fingers curled into his shirt, and she looked up into his eyes. "Promise?"

"Promise." Nash gathered her close.

Londyn's body melted into his.

He held her as she cried, his heart breaking for her.

Londyn had lost her grandfather, the one person

SAVING LONDYN

who had made her feel safe. Now, she'd lost her beloved horse.

How many acres did the rancher own? Nash had heard someone say it was more than fourteen thousand acres. He couldn't even fathom what that looked like or how hard it could be to find a single horse loose on that large of a spread.

He didn't know how they'd do it, but Nash had to find that horse if it was the last thing he did. He'd promised.

145

CHAPTER 9

LONDYN HADN'T CRIED when her grandfather had died, nor had she cried at his funeral. She'd held it together through it all, though it had hurt like someone had ripped her heart out of her chest.

Throwing herself into the spring roundup had allowed her to postpone her grief. She'd worked from early in the morning to late at night, falling into bed too exhausted to think. Then, learning she might lose the ranch had occupied her mind so completely that she wouldn't let herself think about the empty room at the end of the hall in the ranch house.

She hadn't slowed down long enough to process her loss until Butterscotch ran off.

Her grandfather had given her Butterscotch as a newly weaned filly six years ago. They'd worked together to train her. He'd been so proud of how she'd cared for the mare and how well she'd trained her.

Losing Butterscotch was like losing her grandfather all over again.

Because she'd had to take on the responsibility of the ranch, managing the everyday activities and the annual roundup, she hadn't been able to afford appearing weak in front of the ranch hands.

Now, away from LJ Ranch, away from the ranch hands who expected her to be strong like her grandfather and cocooned in Nash's arms, Londyn couldn't hold back. The grief of losing Gramps, the fear of potentially losing her home and the stress of performing for the first time in her life all came to a head with the loss of Butterscotch.

For a handful of minutes, she ugly-cried, her tears soaking Nash's T-shirt.

He stood still, his arms around her, holding her until she'd cried herself out.

Yeah, she could have cried longer, but crying wouldn't get her horse back.

As she surfaced from her grief, she lifted her head. "How?"

He looked down into her eyes, still holding her close. "How what?"

"How are we going to find her?"

He looked over her shoulder in the direction the mare had run. "We need to get to the rancher who owns this place. He would be the best one to help as he's the most familiar with the land and places the mare might go."

She nodded. "And he might have horses or ATVs we can use to search."

"Exactly," Nash concurred. "Let's get to the owner and back here as soon as possible. The longer we're away from this location, the further the mare can go."

Londyn nodded. Still, she hesitated, looking up into his eyes. "Thanks."

"For what?"

Her mouth twisted into a wry grin. "For letting me soak your shirt."

"It'll dry." He brushed his thumb across her damp cheek. "Are you okay now?"

She nodded. "I think so."

"Then let's get moving." He brushed his lips across hers, then stepped back, took her hand and walked to the truck with her. He opened and held the passenger door.

She frowned for a moment.

"I'll drive so you can be looking out for Butter-scotch," he said.

She nodded. "Right." Londyn climbed into the passenger seat and stared out at the vast grasslands. "She could be anywhere."

"We'll find her," he said.

"Yes," she said, squaring her shoulders. "We will." She spoke the words, hoping it would happen if she said them often enough.

Nash closed her door and walked the long way around to the back of the trailer.

In the side mirror, Londyn caught glimpses of Nash as he closed the metal door of the horse trailer and secured the latch.

A sob lodged in Londyn's throat. Butterscotch was gone. Gramps was gone.

Who next?

She shook her head and was still shaking it when Nash climbed into the driver's seat.

He glanced her way, started the truck's engine and shifted into drive. "I looked in the back of the trailer and didn't see anything that would've spooked the mare that badly."

Londyn stared ahead. "I've never seen her do anything like that. It was as if she'd temporarily lost her sanity. It's not like her to lose her shit in the trailer or anywhere else. I raised her from a baby. She's the calmest horse I've ever worked with."

"Once we locate her, we'll have to get a vet to check her out." Nash pressed his foot to the accelerator, easing the truck and trailer forward on the gravel road, slowly increasing its speed.

A mile and a half later, they pulled up next to one of the production equipment trailers.

A group of people had gathered around a tall man with salt-and-pepper gray hair who was wearing blue jeans, a chambray shirt and a cowboy hat.

Nash shifted into park and climbed down from the driver's seat.

Londyn met him at the front of the truck. "That's the rancher, Dan Mitchell. I met him when he came to the set a few days ago to talk with Haynes."

"Good," Nash said. "We'll speak with him first thing."

They marched to the group of people, stopping in front of the rancher.

"Mr. Mitchell," Londyn said. "We met a few days ago. I'm Londyn Tyler-Lovejoy. We need your help."

He nodded. "I remember you. How can I help?"

After Londyn explained what had happened, Mitchell called out to one of his ranch hands. The man hurried over to him. They led Londyn and Nash to a barn, pushed open a large sliding door and strode inside.

Londyn stepped into the semi-dark interior of the barn, allowing her vision to adjust to the limited lighting.

Mitchell walked to a line of ATVs parked at the back of the barn. "Hop on. We'll need to find the mare before that storm gets here. It's moving faster than the weatherman predicted. Fortunately, your director postponed the cattle drive until tomorrow."

Londyn pressed a hand to her chest, where her heart thundered against her ribs. At least she didn't have to worry that she was holding up the film schedule. She slung a leg over the nearest ATV, studied the controls for a moment and then pressed the start button. The engine chugged several times and then engaged, roaring to life.

Nash mounted the ATV beside Londyn's and fired up the engine.

Mitchell and his ranch hand were first out of the barn.

Londyn followed the ranch hand, and Nash followed her.

Mitchell led the way back down the gravel road they'd arrived on.

Londyn drove her ATV up to ride abreast of the rancher. When she got to the spot on the road where they'd opened the trailer, she rolled to a stop and pointed. "Butterscotch is a buckskin mare. She went that way."

Mitchell nodded. "If she goes far enough, she'll run into a creek where she can get water."

"She was acting strange," Londyn said. "Butterscotch is usually well-mannered and calm. It was as if she'd gone berserk."

Mitchell shook his head. "Let's find her. Then we can figure out what happened to make her run."

The four riders spread out and raced across the huge field of gently rolling hills. At about the point Butterscotch had disappeared, the slope dipped down into a narrow valley, explaining why the horse had disappeared so quickly.

Mitchell arrived at a creek bank, stopped and dismounted.

Londyn and Nash pulled their ATVs up to Mitchell's.

Mitchell's ranch hand drove further down the creek bank before he stopped and dismounted.

The rancher dropped to his haunches beside the creek and stared at the ground. "We need to look up and down the length of the creek for hoof prints. As dry as the pastures are, it will be harder to see them there."

They spread out, walking several hundred yards up and down the creek bank.

Nash stuck with Londyn, heading upstream.

Mitchell worked his way back toward where the ranch hand had parked his ATV.

The further they walked, the more desperate Londyn felt. "What if we don't find hoof prints? The T-Bar-M Ranch is over ten thousand acres. It could take days to locate her."

"We'll keep looking." Nash reached for her hand and held it as they walked along the creek.

Londyn appreciated the strength in his touch and the confidence in his tone. But what if they didn't find Butterscotch?

"Over here!" A voice called out in the distance.

Londyn let go of Nash's hand and spun.

The ranch hand waved his arm.

Mitchell squatted at his feet, staring at the ground.

Her heart pounding against her ribs, Londyn ran toward the two men.

Nash kept pace, his gait hampered by a bit of a limp.

When they made it to their ATVs, they mounted and continued toward Mitchell and his ranch hand.

As they approached Mitchell, he straightened to his full height and glanced across the creek.

Londyn slowed to a stop, killed the engine and jumped off the four-wheeler. "What is it?" Londyn asked.

Mitchell pointed at the mud at the edge of the stream. "Hoof prints." Then he pointed to the opposite side of the stream where the bank rose sharply. More hoof prints, some of them smeared as if the horse slid on her way up the bank.

Londyn glanced beyond the opposite bank to more pastureland, empty of animals. Especially empty of one buckskin mare.

Her heart squeezed hard in her chest.

Nash touched her shoulder. "Come on. Let's cross."

She swallowed the lump in her throat and nodded.

"Go on," Mitchell said. "We'll catch up."

Londyn turned and mounted her four-wheeler.

Nash crossed the creek first, gunning the throttle

to make it up the steep bank on the other side. He pulled far enough forward and waited for Londyn.

Familiar with ATVs on her own ranch, she drove down into the streambed, splashing water up on both sides. Then she twisted the throttle, giving it enough gas to blast up the other side. Near the top, the back wheels slipped sideways in the mud.

Londyn leaned forward and pushed on. The front tires grabbed the rim of the bank and launched her over the top. Her heart racing, she slowed as she neared Nash.

"You okay?" he called out.

She nodded and kept going, heading across the grassland with no idea where the mare might have gone.

Mitchell caught up with them and pulled ahead with the ranch hand. He waved his arm to the side, indicating that they should spread out as before, covering a wider swath of land than if they went single-file.

The grassland seemed to extend a long way, with a massive hill rising in the distance. Trees lined the base of the hill and climbed the sides.

If Butterscotch was in those trees, they'd have a hell of a time seeing her. Londyn hoped that whatever had gotten the mare so upset would have worn off by the time she reached the hill. Maybe then, she'd come when she heard her name called.

Clouds built on the western horizon, roiling

upward, blocking the bright sun they'd started the day with.

A flash of lightning lit up the clouds from within.

Londyn couldn't hear thunder with the roar of the four-wheeler engine in her ears. Time was running out. If they didn't find Butterscotch soon, they'd be caught out in the storm. If that were the case, Londyn wouldn't give up.

She might be forced to stop her search when darkness made it impossible to go on. Already, daylight had been cut down to a faded dusk with the clouds blocking the sun. Once the sun actually set, they'd be thrown into the blackest of nights with no stars or moon to light their way.

They'd either have to call it a night and head back to the ranch soon or hunker down and survive the storm in place. None of them were dressed for cold, wet weather. If hypothermia didn't kill them, there was always the chance of being struck by the wicked amount of lightning that accompanied storms on the Wyoming prairie.

If they were forced to postpone the search, what would happen to her mare?

As close as they were to Yellowstone National Park, they were that close to the packs of wolves that had been re-introduced to the area. They had better night vision than humans. A lone horse might be easy pickings for a healthy pack.

Tears welled in Londyn's eyes. No. Absolutely

not. Butterscotch couldn't spend the night alone, unprotected and terrified.

There was no other choice.

They had to find her mare in the next thirty minutes.

Londyn leaned forward, pushing the ATV as fast as she could manage on the bumpy ground. As they neared the tree line, movement caught her eyes.

Dusk made it difficult to distinguish the movement in the dark shadows of the trees. A flash of cream appeared and then disappeared.

"There!" she yelled and took her hand off one handle long enough to point at the position where she'd seen the flash of cream. Londyn gripped the handle and gunned the throttle, shooting forward at breakneck speed. Every bump she hit threatened to unseat her. Twice, she was nearly thrown from her seat. Twice, she regained control and remained on course.

As she neared the tree line, she slowed, peering into the shadows. The flash of cream was nowhere to be seen.

Deep disappointment hit the pit of her belly.

A flash of lightning was quickly followed by a rumbling thunder that reverberated for several seconds.

Londyn stopped her ATV, killed the engine and walked to the edge of the trees. "Butterscotch!" she shouted.

The other ATVs stopped short of the tree line several hundred yards from where Londyn stood. Their engines made it hard to hear anything. If Butterscotch actually heard Londyn's call and responded, Londyn wouldn't hear her answering whinny.

Nash killed his engine, leaped from the seat onto his feet and hurried over to where Londyn stood. "Did you see something?" he asked, his voice low, almost a whisper.

Londyn frowned. "I think I saw a flash cream in the tree shadows." She shrugged. "I could be wrong."

"Call out her name," Nash urged.

"I did, but she might not be able to hear it over the noise of the other engines."

"Keep calling," Nash said.

"Butterscotch!" Londyn yelled and then shook her head. "I can't hear anything. The other engines are echoing off the hill."

"I'll take care of that." Nash ran toward the other two men who sat on their ATVs, looking up at the tree-covered hillside. "Hey!" he yelled, waving his arms.

When Mitchell finally turned toward him, Nash stopped and sliced his hand across his throat. "Cut the engines!" he yelled, knowing they couldn't possibly hear him. He made a slicing motion across his throat again.

Mitchell turned off his ATV.

The ranch hand followed suit.

Lightning flashed overhead.

Londyn counted in her head.

One thousand and one... One thousand and two... One thousand and three... One thousand and four... One thousand and—

Thunder cracked the sky and rumbled on for several long moments. The lightning had struck almost a mile away. They were definitely in the danger zone of being struck by lightning.

Nash hurried back to her. "We need to get out of here."

"You're right," she said. "You should go and take the other two with you. It's too dangerous to be out in a lightning storm."

He frowned. "What about you?"

She shook her head, her gaze combing through the shadows beneath the trees. "She's in there. I'm not leaving without her. But there's no reason for you three to stay."

"The hell there isn't," Nash said. "If you're staying, I'm staying."

"Just stand away from me," she said. "You're taller than I am. Lightning is drawn to taller targets."

Nash snorted and chuckled. "You're a piece of work, Miss Tyler-Lovejoy."

"And this is news to you?" she said with a cocked eyebrow. "I'm surprised my mother didn't tell you what to expect."

"Oh, she did," he said. "Your horse's name is Butterscotch?"

She nodded.

"Butterscotch!" he yelled and paused to listen.

Londyn heard nothing.

"Maybe she'll come to your voice," he suggested.

She nodded and yelled, "Butterscotch!"

Again, nothing moved in the shadows.

Lightning flashed.

Londyn counted. Four seconds.

When Nash drew a deep breath to yell again, Londyn laid a hand on his arm and shook her head.

"Let me try something that works when she's out in the pasture." She raised her fingers to her lips and emitted a long, piercing whistle.

They stood for a long moment, listening for the thunder of horse's hooves.

The only thunder Londyn heard was from the sky.

Another flash of lightning nearly blinded them. Thunder followed immediately.

Nash cupped her elbow. "Come on, Londyn. We need to get back to the ranch before we're struck by lightning."

She pulled free of his grip, shaking her head. "You go. I'm not going anywhere until I find my horse."

"I have no way to protect you from—"

"Shhh." A sound captured Londyn's attention. She touched Nash's arm. "Did you hear that?"

His eyes narrowed. "No."

Londyn strained to hear anything. The sound came again.

"There," Londyn said. "Did you hear that?"

"Maybe," he said, his brow furrowing.

Her pulse whipped into high gear as she peered into the tree line. Something moved in the shadows. "Did you see that?"

"Yes."

"Butterscotch!" Londyn yelled. "I'm here, girl!"

She started toward the trees.

Nash caught up to her and grabbed her arm. "What if it's not the horse? It could be a wolf or a bear." He pulled his pistol out of the holster beneath his jacket.

"That won't stop a bear," Londyn said. "And it's Butterscotch. I just know it."

"You'd bet your life on it?" he asked, refusing to release her arm.

She nodded. "It has to be her." Londyn lifted her fingers to her lips again and blew out another sharp whistle.

An answering whinny echoed through the tree trunks.

Moments later, Butterscotch raced down a hill-side and out from beneath the trees, running straight for Londyn.

CHAPTER 10

NASH STEPPED between Londyn and the oncoming horse.

Londyn gripped his arm. "It's okay. She'll stop for me." Before he could stop her, she moved around him as the buckskin mare slid to a stop in front of her.

She grabbed the horse's lead and touched her hand to her velvety-soft nose. "There you are, big girl. It's okay. We're going to be okay," she spoke as tears ran down her face.

The mare was breathing hard, and her coat was lathered in sweat, but her eyes weren't wild, and her nostrils weren't flaring like they had when she'd broken free of the trailer. Hopefully, whatever had gotten into her had passed.

A big drop of rain splattered across Nash's forehead, followed by another and another.

They had to get Butterscotch to shelter. Fast.

Lightning struck a tree nearby with a loud crack and an ear-splitting boom of thunder.

Butterscotch reared.

Because she was holding tightly to the lead, Londyn's feet left the ground as the horse rose.

Nash grabbed her around the waist and pulled her backward as Butterscotch came down on all four hooves.

Nash released her waist and reached for the lead, his hands closing over Londyn's. Together, they brought the mare to a standstill.

The ranch owner and his ranch hand drove their ATVs close to where Nash and Londyn stood with the mare. "Let's get her back to the ranch," Mitchell said.

"How do you want to do this?" Nash asked. "I can ride her bareback."

Londyn shook her head. "No. I've led her behind an ATV before. She'll follow as long as we keep moving."

Nash's brow dipped low. "You're not going to hold the lead, are you?"

Londyn nodded her head, brushing the raindrops out over her eyes. "I have to. If we try to tie it to the back of the ATV, she might spook and hurt herself trying to get away from it. The best thing would be to walk her all the way back."

"It's too far," Mitchell said. "This storm isn't waiting for anyone."

As if to demonstrate, the big drops increased in quantity until it was hard to see three feet in front of his nose. Nash shook his head. "We can't walk all the way back."

Londyn's lips pressed into a stubborn line. "I'll walk her all the way if I have to. She's been through enough."

"Look," Mitchell said. "Get her back out to the road. I'll go ahead and bring your truck and trailer closer. That way, you won't be walking all night."

"Ok," Nash said. "We'll get there as quickly as possible."

Mitchell climbed onto his ATV, turned on the headlight and headed across the field. The sheets of rain smudged the light until it finally disappeared into the darkness.

The ranch hand mounted his four-wheeler. "Leave the other ATVs here. We'll come back for them after the storm. I'll lead you back to the road." He took off, riding slowly, a little ahead of them.

"You should ride one of the ATVs," Londyn said. "I can handle Butterscotch."

Nash shook his head. "I'm walking with you."

Londyn didn't argue, apparently too tired and emotionally wrung out. She fell in step beside him, walking as fast as she could. Rain pelted her face and soaked her all the way through her denim jacket to her skin. She shivered and wiped the water from her eyes, only to have to do it again immediately.

Nash's heart pinched in his chest. The woman was far too stubborn to ask for help.

Nash shrugged out of his leather jacket and draped it over her shoulders.

"No," she said. "You need it to stay dry."

He shook his head. "I'm fine. I was getting hot."

"You're lying," Londyn muttered. "But I appreciate the gesture, and I'm too cold to fight you on this one."

"Good," he said and hooked her arm. "Then let's get going."

She walked as fast as she could, obviously anxious to get Butterscotch back to the ranch and hopefully into a dry stall for the night. "I'm sorry you're stuck in this situation. I'm sure you didn't sign up for a trek in the cold rain with lightning striking all around."

"I've been in worse," he said.

Several times along the way, the lightning strikes and ensuing thunder made the mare rear.

Each time, Nash helped Londyn calm the animal and keep her moving.

When they reached the creek, the ranch hand blew through quickly, nearly stalling out when he sank up to his hips in water. He barely managed to make it to the other side. When he did, he turned his ATV around and shined the light down at the creek.

"I'll take Butterscotch across and come back for you," Nash said.

"I can do it," Londyn said.

"Please," he insisted. "Stay here. I'll be right back."

She stood at the top of the creek bank, unused to standing back and letting someone else do what she could have done herself. As the man and horse stepped over the edge, Londyn held her breath.

Nash led the mare down the steep bank, both slipping precariously in the mud.

When they reached the creek bed, the water rose around them. Butterscotch had no problem navigating the rush of water. For Nash, it was a little more of a struggle. The creek had gone from nothing more than a trickle to knee-deep and rushing with the rain runoff.

Nash struggled, had his feet swept out from under him, caught himself on Butterscotch's halter and made it the rest of the way across.

He handed the lead to the ranch hand and slid down the bank into the creek. After making sure he was steady, he waded slowly through the rushing water and climbed the slippery creek bank to stand beside her.

With rain running down her face, Londyn shook her head.

Nash slung mud off his hands as best he could, then held one out to her.

She took it, mud and all.

As soon as they carefully stepped over the edge, their feet flew out from under them. They slid down the bank and into the stream.

By that time, the flow had become a raging river. Nash and Londyn were swept away.

Londyn fought to keep her head above water, with Nash holding her hand in a vice-like grip.

All she could see in the occasional moment with her head above the surface, was the light shining into the creek further upstream where they were supposed to have crossed.

They'd gone several yards down the river when she was yanked to a halt by that grip on her hand. Waves rushed over her head for so long she thought for sure she would drown. Then, the grip on her hand tightened. She was pulled up and out of the water onto a tree branch growing out of the side of the bank.

Nash pulled her up onto a thicker branch and into his arms.

"Are you all right?" he yelled about the roar of the river, his arm tightening around her.

Londyn coughed the water from her lungs and wrapped her arms around his waist. "I am now."

He held her close, his arms like vices around her.

Londyn was so cold she couldn't tell who was shaking more.

A light above their heads bounced toward them. When it finally came abreast of where they clung to the tree, it shined down on them.

When they could finally see the tree branches, Nash loosened his hold on Londyn and helped her climb the limbs ahead of him, following, ready to catch her should she slip and fall back.

Londyn finally made it to level ground, out of the creek and away from the slippery bank.

Before she could ask, the ranch hand said, "Don't worry. The mare is tied to a tree." He led them back to Butterscotch.

Exhausted from their impromptu swim and attempted drowning, Londyn trudged along beside her horse, glad for the halter to hold onto when her knees buckled or she tripped over a rock or stubby vegetation.

What felt like hours later, they arrived at the road where the truck and trailer waited.

Mitchell and two more of his ranch hands took charge of Butterscotch. The mare walked right up into the trailer without a problem.

Londyn climbed into the back seat, wet, muddy and so cold her teeth chattered.

Nash slid in beside her, pulled her into his arms and held her all the way to the ranch house. Having almost lost her in the raging creek had shaken him more than he could have imagined.

As they rolled into the barnyard, Nash frowned.

Though the equipment vans were still parked in front of the barn, many of the other vehicles belonging to the cast and crew were gone.

"Where did everybody go?" Londyn asked.

"Your director sent them. Apparently, a lightning

strike took out one of their primary generators and some of the camera equipment. A couple of your cast members decided to stay the night rather than risk driving back in the rain. The rest returned to your film location. You can get all the details from those who stayed behind."

Nash helped Londyn down from the truck and slipped an arm around her as they walked to the rear to open the trailer.

Butterscotch stood in the front compartment, her head drooping. Londyn climbed in and stopped beside the mare's neck. "Hey, girl," she said softly. "Rough night?"

The mare tossed her head.

"Yeah. I know." Londyn stroked the mare's nose. "We're going to get you to a dry stall with lovely hay and grain." She gripped the halter and slowly backed the animal down the ramp.

"I had one of my guys prepare a stall for the mare," Mitchell said. "Follow me." He led the way into the barn.

An older man in overalls stood beside an open stall door with an armful of ragged towels.

Once Londyn led Butterscotch into the stall, the man handed her a towel.

Nash took half of the remaining towels.

Together, Nash and Londyn rubbed the horse down while she drank from a water bucket. The stall's floor had been lined with fresh woodchips.

Someone had filled the feed trough with grain and fresh alfalfa hay.

Mitchell leaned against the open stall door. "I called my vet. He's on his way out. Based on your description of the horse's behavior, he suspects she got into something that triggered a reaction. He wants to take a blood sample and have it tested."

"Thank you." Londyn peered over the top of her horse's back. "I've never seen her so distressed. However, I can't imagine what she could have gotten into. I had her in a portable corral. I've fed her nothing but hay and grain from my ranch."

Mitchell shrugged. "People can be careless—especially those who aren't around horses often. I've had a guest give one of my horses whiskey, thinking that was funny. That horse was sick for days."

They'd barely gotten the horse dried off when she shifted impatiently.

Londyn and Nash moved toward the stall door.

Butterscotch bent her front legs and lowered her rear, laying down in the bed of wood chips.

"She didn't eat any of the feed or hay," Londyn said.

"She probably just needs time to recover from whatever triggered her." Nash could see the worry in Londyn's eyes and wished he could do something to make her feel better. Even more so, he wished he could do something to make the horse feel better.

"I have a couple of guest rooms in the ranch house

prepared for you," Mitchell said. "You're welcome to stay with us."

Londyn shook her head. "If it's all right by you, I'd like to sleep out here with Butterscotch."

Mitchell shrugged. "It's your call. I get it. I'd do the same."

Nash nodded. "We'll both be out here for the night."

"I'll have some sleeping bags brought out. If the clouds clear, it'll get cold."

"Thanks," Nash said.

"Yes," Londyn said. "We'll try not to be too much of a bother."

"Don't worry about it," Mitchell said with a grin. "The movie studio is paying us a lot to use my cattle and the ranch for filming the cattle drive. It'll help pad my bank account for the winter months."

"I'm glad to hear that," Londyn said. "Winter months can be hard."

Mitchell nodded. "You should know. You're even further north than we are."

Londyn smiled. "Not by much. That jet stream can be brutal in January and February, dipping down into Wyoming."

"Where's my patient?" A man appeared in the doorway of the barn carrying a satchel. He folded an umbrella, set it by the door and shrugged out of a rain jacket. The man wore jeans and a stained and rumpled denim shirt. He had dark circles beneath his eyes and fine lines at the corners.

"Hey, Doc." Mitchell stepped back, making room for the veterinarian to enter the stall. "Thanks for making the trip out, especially in such bad weather."

"I was in your neighborhood over at the Taylor's ranch with a breech calf," the doctor said. "Otherwise, I would've asked you to wait until morning." He glanced toward Nash and Londyn. "I'm Dr. Matheson."

Nash held out his hand. "Nash Nelson. And this is Londyn Tyler-Lovejoy, the horse's owner."

Londyn shook the vet's hand. "Please, call me Londyn." She stepped out of the stall doorway and waved toward the buckskin. "This is Butterscotch."

Dr. Matheson squatted beside Butterscotch and laid his hand on her neck. "How long has she been down?"

Londyn knelt beside the vet. "She just laid down." She explained what had happened and how the horse had gone berserk. "I've never seen her do that before. She's the calmest horse I've ever worked with. It was as if she'd suddenly lost her mind."

The veterinarian gave the horse a quick exam, checking her eyes, teeth, gums and heartbeat. Then he plucked a syringe out of his satchel and drew blood. "I'll send the sample out to be tested. The results won't be available for a couple of days."

"I'd like to get her back to my ranch to recuperate," Londyn said. "It's about a two-hour drive from here."

"I'd give her something to counteract an allergic reaction, but she's calm and breathing normally. She doesn't seem to be distressed at this time." He straightened. "If she's up and acting fairly normal by morning, she should be all right to transport. She might feel better in familiar surroundings."

Londyn scratched behind Butterscotch's ear and patted her neck. When she stood, she shook the veterinarian's hand. "Thank you for coming out."

"My pleasure." He lifted his chin toward the ranch owner. "Dan tells me you're a member of the cast shooting the movie on his place in the park. I look forward to watching it on the big screen." He shook her hand. "I'll get back with the results as soon as possible. And I'll be on call during the filming to look after the health and well-being of the other animals."

"That's good to hear," Londyn said. "Be careful driving home in this storm."

"Thanks. I will." Dr. Matheson gave them a nod, gripped the handle of his satchel and left the barn.

The veterinarian pulled on his rain jacket, popped open his umbrella and left. As he exited, one of Mitchell's men entered the barn, carrying two trash bags. He opened the bags one at a time and pulled out two tightly bound sleeping bags.

"Oh, good," Mitchell pointed to the bags. "They're not mattresses with fresh sheets and pillows, but they'll keep you warm. If you change your minds and want to come to the house, just knock on the front door. Our dogs bark loud enough to wake the dead."

"I'm sure the bags will be fine," Londyn said.

"The stall next to this one was thoroughly cleaned, disinfected and has fresh woodchips," Mitchell offered. "You can be nearby if needed, but not stepped on, should your horse get up in the night."

"Perfect," Londyn said.

"I'll have my cook send out some sandwiches. He baked a huge ham for our guests and ranch hands. There was a lot left."

Nash's stomach rumbled loudly in response to the mention of a ham sandwich. He laughed. "That would be great. You sure it's not too much trouble?"

Londyn elbowed him in the side. "Shh. He's offering food." She smiled. "We'd love a sandwich."

Mitchell chuckled. "Cookie won't mind. He loves it when we have guests, even if they choose to stay in the barn. I'll also bring out some dry clothes for you two to change into. You can't stay in your wet things all night."

Nash smiled. "There's no need for anyone else to get out in this storm. We can come to the house to get the food and clothing since we're already soaked."

"I insist." Mitchell nodded toward Londyn. "My sister is about your size. She leaves work clothes here for when she visits from Seattle. I'm sure I can find something for both of you. It might be half an hour or so, depending on what I can find in our closets."

"We'll be fine until then," Londyn said. "Thank you for everything."

Mitchell stepped back out into the storm.

Londyn shrugged out of Nash's leather jacket. "I hope the rain doesn't ruin your coat." She hung it on a hook outside the stall door. "Thank you for letting me use it."

"It's been wet before. It'll be fine when it dries." He stepped back into the stall with Butterscotch and scooped a handful of feed out of the trough, knelt and offered it to the horse.

She sniffed and then nuzzled his palm, taking his offering.

"I'm glad she's eating something," Londyn said. "She'd probably exhausted from her wild escape."

"Probably." Nash rose and grabbed another handful of grain and offered it to the mare. She ate that little bit as well. It reassured Nash for the moment. "I wouldn't worry too much about her unless she doesn't get up in the morning."

"Right." Londyn chewed on her bottom lip as she stared down at the mare. "I can't imagine what caused her to freak out."

"Let's hope the blood test will give us a clue."

Londyn nodded, her gaze shifting to Nash. "Thank you for saving me from being swept away in the creek."

"Just doing my job," he said. "What kind of protector would I be if I let a little flooded creek carry you away?" His mouth pressed into a thin line. "But seriously, I'm sorry I let you get swept away at all."

She laid a hand on his shoulder. "If you hadn't been there, Butterscotch and I might not have made it across that creek."

He stared at the horse nibbling the grain from his palm. He laid his other hand over hers on his shoulder without saying a word. Despite the electric shock, or maybe because of the sensation, he held onto that hand longer than he should have.

Having almost lost her in the raging floodwaters, he wanted to hold on and keep holding on.

Nash curled his fingers around hers and gently pulled her around to stand in front of him.

"This might sound stupid, or maybe even like a pathetic excuse for a pickup line, but I have to say it."

Her lips lifted in a smile. "Now you have my full attention. Say what's on your mind." She brushed a lock of his hair off his forehead.

He drew in a deep breath and let it out slowly. "We haven't known each other long, but for some reason, I feel like I've known you forever. I've lost friends. One minute, they're there; the next, they're gone. For a moment back there, I almost lost you."

"But you didn't," she said and brushed her lips across his forehead. "You saved my life."

He shook his head. "A tree saved our lives. If I hadn't run into it, we wouldn't have survived much longer. The tree saved us."

She grasped his cheeks between her hands. "No," she said. "You saved our lives. Your quick thinking and strength got us out of that creek."

He let go of her hand, gripped her hips and pulled her into his lap, burying his face against her neck. "I promise to do better," he said. "I can't let you die."

She slid her hands behind his neck and pulled him close to where their lips almost met. "I'm not going to die." Her lips brushed his softly. "I'm not going to die."

"You almost did," he whispered against her mouth.

"I'm a lot tougher than you think."

"Don't you see?" He gripped her head, his fingers sinking into her damp hair. "It isn't always how strong, fast or tough you are. I want—" He crushed his mouth to hers, drinking her in like a man who'd been in a desert too long.

She opened to him.

His tongue met hers, stroking the length, caressing with a passion borne of desperation.

He'd almost lost her. It could have been Waterson all over again. There one minute. Dead the next, in a ground-rocking explosion.

The barn door creaked open.

Lightning flashed, the lights overhead blinked out

and thunder boomed like a grenade detonating, shaking the very ground on which they sat.

Nash froze.

"Holy shit!" A male voice exclaimed. A beam of light splashed through the barn's interior, a glowing stream crossing in front of the open stall door. "Hello?"

Before he could stop her, Londyn scrambled off Nash's lap. "Hang on." She stepped out of the stall. "We're in here."

Nash was on his feet and at her side in seconds.

A man wearing a rain slicker carried a flashlight and a backpack. "I'm Cookie," he said. "I take it you're our guests with the sick horse?"

"Yes, sir," Londyn said. "I'm Londyn, and this is Nash."

"Nice to meet you," Cookie said. He set the flashlight on the ground and slid the backpack off his shoulders. "I brought you sandwiches, a thermos of hot cocoa and some clothes Mitch dug out of his closets. I'd have brought you coffee, but you might want to sleep at least some of the night."

Cookie pulled a gallon-sized plastic baggie and a thermos out of the backpack. Then he pulled out a garbage bag. "These are the clothes."

Nash hurried toward the man and took the bags and thermos from him. "Thank you."

"Helluva storm out there," the man said, switching the flashlight to his other hand once it was free. He glanced at the ceiling of the barn. "Hopefully, the lights will come back on in a few minutes. But, just in case they don't, there's a spare flashlight in the tack room. I'll get it for you. Hang on."

Nash wanted to tell the man they weren't going anywhere in the pitch black.

Cookie disappeared with the light beam into a room in the front corner of the barn. A moment later, he reappeared, carrying something that appeared to be a lantern. "This is even better than a flashlight. It's battery-powered, so you don't have to worry about it catching the hay on fire." He set it on the ground, shined his flashlight down at the base of the unit, located the switch and turned it on.

Light glowed in a warm circle around them, breaking up the darkness.

"There. Hopefully, the battery will last all night or at least until the electricity comes back on." Cookie grinned. "Need anything else?"

Nash shook his head, willing the older man to leave so they could pick up where he and Londyn had left off. He could still taste her on his lips and wanted more.

Cookie clapped his hands together. "Then I'm off to bed. Breakfast is at six-thirty. You can come through the kitchen door at the back of the house. Be on time so you actually get some food. The ranch hands don't leave so much as a scrap." He nodded.

"Good night. I hope your horse is feeling better by morning."

The older man ducked back out into the storm, closing the door behind him and leaving Nash and Londyn in the warm glow of the lantern.

Nash set the bag of clothes in the stall beside the one with Butterscotch. He laid the plastic baggie full of sandwiches and the thermos on top of the clothes.

When he turned, he found Londyn in the stall doorway behind him, holding the lantern. Once she had his attention, she entered and set the lantern on the floor. When she straightened, the lantern glow reflected in her dark eyes as she closed the distance between them.

For a long moment, she stood before him. "Are you hungry?" she asked in almost a whisper.

Though his stomach had rumbled moments before, he's lost all appetite for food. "I find I'm not hungry for ham, but I have an insatiable appetite for you."

Her dark eyes flared, but she didn't walk into his arms. "Can we agree that you have your work, and I have my ranch? They could, in fact, be mutually exclusive?"

Nash's brow dipped low. "Agree?"

She nodded. "And can we agree that anything that happens between us tonight doesn't have to mean anything? We'll go our separate ways when the filming is complete?"

"Is that what you want?" he asked.

She nodded. "What we're feeling is a product of trauma. It won't last. Especially when I'll go back to my ranch, and you'll go on to your next assignment. We live vastly different lives. Why complicate them?"

He gathered her into his arms. "Sweetheart, it's too late."

Her breathing grew ragged as she stared up at him. "Too late?" she whispered as if she didn't have enough breath to push words past her vocal cords.

He nodded. "Everything about this..." he cupped her cheek and brushed his thumb across her lips, "... is complicated."

Her lips puckered, kissing his thumb. "It doesn't have to...be," she said.

He stood still, holding onto his control by a thread. "The only way to keep from getting more complicated is to stop now."

Her eyes widened. "Please," she said, "don't," she sucked in a breath, "stop."

Londyn leaned up on her toes and pressed her lips to his.

That thread snapped.

Nash pulled her into his arms and deepened the kiss, taking all she wanted to give and more.

They were about to take complicated to a whole new level.

CHAPTER 11

LONDYN HAD NEARLY DIED several times in the past couple of days, but nothing felt as close to transcending to heaven as that kiss.

For years, she'd thought herself cold, passionless and unable to feel deeply about other humans besides her family.

Until she'd met Nash.

From the moment he'd insisted on taking over her protection, she'd been at once annoyed and frustrated. Perhaps that had been why she'd instinctively pushed back, insisting she didn't need him.

Had her body recognized what her mind had refused to see? That this man could ignite within her core an inferno so hot nothing could extinguish the flame?

She fell into the man, giving everything she had to that kiss, desperately clinging to him as if her life depended on it. Just like it had as she'd clung to his hand in the raging river.

He stepped behind her and closed the stall door. Not that it gave them complete privacy. The stall doors only rose five feet from the ground. Anyone could walk into the barn, peer over the top of the door and see what was going on inside.

Rather than make her want to stop, the idea of someone catching them in the act was titillating, almost dangerous.

Nash broke the kiss and stepped away, his gaze holding hers. Then he grabbed one of the sleeping bags and untied the strap holding it in a tight roll. Grasping the end, he flicked his wrist, popping the bag open.

Londyn reached for the zipper and quickly ran it all the way down the length, around the corner and freed the width. She took one end. Nash held the other, and they stretched the bag out, laying it over the bed of woodchips.

They worked quickly together to spread out the other sleeping bag and laid it over the first.

"I'm going to check on Butterscotch," Nash said.

A stab of guilt hit her in the gut. "I'll do it."

Nash shook his head. "Let me. It'll give you time to get out of those wet clothes and find something in the items Mitchell sent."

For a moment, Londyn hesitated.

He held up a hand as if swearing in at a courtroom. "I promise, I'll let you know if she's looking any worse."

Londyn nodded. "Okay."

Nash left, closing the door behind him. The squeal of metal hinges sounded from the next stall.

Londyn strained to hear his murmured words spoken to the mare. Even talking to a horse, he sounded incredibly sexy.

Though her wet clothes chilled her skin, Londyn was heating up inside. She opened the bag of clothing Mitchell had sent and found a sweatshirt with *University of Montana* emblazoned across the front. She also found a pair of sweatpants too short for Nash but just right for her.

Londyn kicked off her boots and quickly stripped out of her wet jeans, shirt and bra, hanging them over the sides of the empty trough to allow them to dry as much as possible before she had to put them back on.

She pulled on the sweatshirt, glad it was oversized and fell to mid-thigh, warming her cool skin.

Hinges squealed again, and Nash's head appeared over the top of the stall door before he pushed it open and stepped inside.

"Butterscotch seems to be doing better. She ate a couple more handfuls of grain."

"Thanks," she said, her voice breathy, as if she couldn't get enough air in her lungs.

His gaze swept over the sweatshirt, down to where the hem brushed across her, mid-thigh.

"You should get out of those wet clothes," she said, her voice shaking. "Dry clothes are much warmer." A rush of intense longing washed over her. If they only had one night together, she had to go for what she wanted.

His eyes narrowed. "To be perfectly clear... Are we going where I think we're going?"

Londyn nodded, her mouth suddenly dry and her pulse hammering through her veins. She moved forward and worked the buttons on his shirt down to where it was tucked into his jeans.

Nash pulled the hem from his waistband.

Londyn pushed the garment over his shoulders and pulled it off, hanging it over the stall door.

Nash unbuckled his belt, toed off his boots and peeled his wet jeans down his legs. Naked, he turned to face her. She took the jeans from him and draped them over the door without actually looking, her gaze otherwise occupied with his gorgeous body and his rigid cock.

"No regrets," she whispered and stepped into his arms, her hands going behind him to cup his tight ass.

Freed from the wet clothes, his skin was cool to her touch but stretched taut over thick muscles.

Immediately, his cock swelled, pressing against the sweatshirt, nudging her belly. His hands swept over her arms and downward, molding the fabric

over her hips, moving lower to slide beneath
the hem.

Londyn's breath caught and held in her throat as
Nash's fingers dug into the flesh of her buttocks and
then slid down to grasp her thighs. As he hoisted her
up, she wrapped her legs around his waist and lowered
herself down until his cock nudged her entrance.

She wanted him inside her more than she wanted
to breathe.

"Wait," he said, cutting through her haze of
passion.

"Wait?" She blinked, her gaze meeting his. "Are
you kidding?"

He chuckled. "Protection?"

Londyn pulled in a deep breath and let it out.
"Right." She unlocked her legs from around his waist.
"Do you have any?"

"I hope so." Nash lifted her off him and set her on
her bare feet on top of the sleeping bags. He grabbed
his jeans from where she'd hung them on the stall
door. When he dug his hand into the back pocket, he
let out a stream of curses.

"What?" Londyn asked.

"My wallet isn't in my pocket." He hung the jeans
back on the door. "It must have fallen out in the
creek."

Londyn shook her head and walked across the
stall to stand beside him. Then she bent and felt

around in the woodchips. "It might have fallen out when I hung your jeans."

While she searched the stall floor, he leaned over the door and stared at the ground on the other side. "There it is," he said.

Londyn straightened with a crooked smile. "Sorry. I didn't realize it was still in your pocket. I was otherwise engaged with the view of your incredible...assets."

Nash chuckled, opened the stall, retrieved the wallet and closed the door again. He dug into the wallet. "I just hope I have—" With a grin, he pulled out a small square packet. "Bingo."

She took the packet and tossed it onto the sleeping bags.

Nash frowned. "But I thought..."

"Ever heard of foreplay?" She grabbed the hem of the sweatshirt and dragged it slowly up her torso, past her breasts and over her head, letting it drop silently to the floor filled with woodchips. Then she took his hand and led him to the makeshift bed.

She was by no means a virgin, but she'd never performed a striptease for a man. Something about Nash and being cocooned in the barn with a storm raging around them made her toss all inhibition to the wild winds blowing against the barn walls. Londyn knelt on the bedding before him.

When he started to lower himself to join her, she shook her head. "Not yet."

His brow dipped.

"First, this." She wrapped her hands around his cock and guided it to her mouth. It was hot and thick. "So hard."

"You do that to me," he said.

She touched her tongue to the tip of his shaft.

He gasped and jerked backward.

Her eyebrows rose. "Don't you like that?"

He drew in a deep breath and let it out slowly. "Too much. I doubt I'll last long."

"I thought you special ops types were known for your tight control."

"On our aim, our focus and our emotions. But this—"

She wrapped her lips around his cock, grasped his buttocks and pulled him in until he bumped against the back of her throat.

"No control. None. Nada." He sucked in a breath and held it as she eased back slowly, twisting her tongue around his shaft.

His fingers threaded through her damp hair and pulled her back over him.

She took all of him and eased off again, rocking back and forth, faster and faster.

His buttocks tightened beneath her fingers, and his hands gripped her head, gently pulling her off him. "I can't hold back much longer," he said through gritted teeth.

"Then don't." She laid back on the sleeping bag,

fumbled for the condom and waited for him to come to her.

For a long moment, he stood over her, his cock engorged, jutting straight out, impossibly large.

Londyn ran her tongue across her lips, the taste of him lingering in her mouth.

Nash shook his head.

Londyn's heart seized. Had he changed his mind? Was she being too eager? Had she turned him off?

"You are..." he said, his voice tight, "...beautiful." Then he dropped to the bedding, leaned over and kissed her so long and so hard she forgot to breathe.

When he relinquished her lips, he traced a path from her mouth to just below her ear and then down the length of her neck to the pulse beating wildly at the base.

Her breathing grew ragged as he moved lower, his hand cupping her breast, plumping it up so that he could take the nipple between his lips and nibble gently.

Her back arched, urging him to take more.

He sucked her tit into his mouth, pulled hard and then flicked the tip with his tongue.

Londyn writhed beneath him, her body undulating with each stroke of his tongue.

Rather than treat the other breast to the same, he worked his way hungrily down her torso to the juncture of her thighs, parting her legs so that he could settle his broad shoulders between them.

Then he took her with his mouth, flicking his tongue across her clit, then swirling it slowly. His fingers found her channel and slipped inside her slick entrance with one, then two, then three fingers, thrusting in and out as he sucked her clit into his mouth, stroking it with his tongue.

Londyn had never felt sensations as intense as she did at that moment. Her hips rocked with every brush of his tongue.

She wove her hands into his hair and held him close, reveling in the electric currents that built with each flick and each stroke. The tension became so powerful she let go of all inhibition and shot into orbit in a release so profound she was sure she'd died and gone to heaven.

Wave after wave washed through her until the tide ebbed, and she fell back to earth. Heavy rain pounded the barn's tin roof, echoing the thundering beat of her heart.

Nash rose on his arms, leaned over and kissed her, the musk of her release on his mouth.

When her senses slowly returned, Londyn realized an overpowering need for more. What he'd started wasn't nearly enough.

"Did you like that?" he asked.

She nodded and then shook her head.

His brow furrowed. "Is that a yes or a no?"

"It's a not enough," she said. "I want more."

He chuckled. "Greedy, are you?"

She nodded, planted her hands on his chest and pushed him off her and onto his back.

Londyn rolled over, straddled his legs and searched the bedding.

"Looking for this?" Nash held up the little square packet.

Londyn snatched it from his hand, tore it open and rolled the condom over his shaft, all the way down to the base. She paused to fondle his balls before rising over him and easing herself onto him.

As his shaft filled her, the air left her lungs. She flung back her head and took all of him into her, his girth stretching her tight channel.

"Sweet Jesus," he murmured. "You feel so damned good."

"I never knew it could feel..." she rose up and lowered onto him again, "... like this."

He let her set the pace for a few moments. Then he gripped her hips and lifted her off him. "I need to drive," he said.

She rolled onto her back and opened her legs to him.

He came into her, thrusting hard and fast, again and again.

Londyn dug her heels into the sleeping bag and pushed upward, meeting his thrusts with ones of her own, forcing him deeper.

Fiery sensations rippled through her as she ascended to the very edge and launched into the stratosphere. Thunder boomed outside in the storm like a crescendo of her orgasm.

Nash dropped down on her, gathered her into his arms and thrust once more, his body going rigid.

For a long, crushing moment, he remained buried inside her, his cock pulsing against her channel.

When Nash rolled to the side, air rushed into Londyn's lungs.

Thunder boomed again, rattling the tin roof.

A frightened whinny sounded from the stall beside them.

Londyn wanted to prolong their intimate connection longer. The mare might just be protesting about the frightening percussion of the storm outside. If Londyn just stayed where she was, the horse would grow calm.

When Butterscotch whinnied again, Londyn sighed.

"I'll check on her." Nash slid out of her and pushed to his feet.

"Let me," Londyn said, scrambling to stand, her legs wobbling.

"We'll do it together," he said and opened the stall door.

"Naked?" Londyn peered around the open door.

"Someone would have to be crazy to be out in this storm." He stepped out of the stall and held out his hand.

A flash of lightning made the overhead lights flicker and then remain on.

Feeling a little self-conscious and a whole lotta wicked, Londyn stepped out of the stall, naked as the day she was born, to stand beside Nash.

His body was gorgeous, the muscles toned and rippling with every movement.

She wanted to touch every inch of him.

He opened the stall door.

Londyn gasped. "You're up," she said, smiling at Butterscotch as she stood with her head in the trough, munching grain and alfalfa.

Londyn stepped into the stall and ran her hand along the mare's neck. "Glad you're feeling better. We're going to take you home in the morning, where you won't have to worry about anything."

The mare turned her head and nuzzled Londyn's breast.

"Hey, save those for me," Nash said.

Londyn laughed, relieved her horse was on her feet. "Glad to see you're eating." She scratched behind the animal's ears and backed out of the stall.

Nash closed the door and latched it. "Speaking of eating..." he said.

Londyn ran her hand over her torso and down to the juncture of her thighs. Her pussy was still deliciously wet and slightly achy. "Are you hungry?"

Nash's eyes flared. "Starving." He swept her into

his arms and carried her back into their stall, where he laid her on the sleeping bags and then kissed her.

She was just raising her arms to wrap around his neck when he jumped up and reached for the bag of sandwiches.

"Seriously? You're that kind of hungry?"

He laughed. "I am. It takes fuel to keep this body moving."

She sat up, her belly rumbling. "Seems a shame to waste the mood."

"Not when you have grapes." He pulled sandwiches out of the bag and handed her one. Then, he held up the bag to display the grapes inside. "Grapes are great for getting back in the mood."

Londyn took the sandwich he proffered. "You'll have to show me."

"Oh, I will," he said with a wink. "But first, we need to eat so we have enough energy to last all night."

Her sandwich poised in front of her lips, Londyn's eyes widened, and heat coiled at her core. "All night?" she whispered.

"I'm not wasting a second with you," he said and leaned across to kiss her lips. "Now, eat. We have grapes waiting for us."

Londyn sank her teeth in the delicious ham sandwich and quickly chewed, anxious to discover what Nash had in mind.

Grapes?

CHAPTER 12

N<small>ASH WOKE BEFORE DAWN</small>, crawled out of the nest they'd made of the sleeping bags and pulled on the jeans and shirt Mitchell had provided. Though he'd also given him dry socks, they were damp within moments of pulling on his waterlogged boots.

It didn't matter. They had a long drive to get to LJ Ranch. The sooner they got started, the better. He could worry about what to do about wet boots when they got there.

Once dressed, he eased open the stall door and peered over the one beside it at Butterscotch standing calmly in the woodchips. As soon as she spotted him, she walked over to the door and hung her head over the top, nuzzling his hand for grain.

"Sorry, sweet girl," he said. "I'll ask for more when the ranch hands come in."

A movement behind him made him turn.

Londyn stood at the door of their stall, pulling on the sweatshirt with University of Montana written across the front.

"Hey," he said.

"Hey, yourself." She gave him a tenuous smile.

He held open his arms, and she walked into them wearing boots just as waterlogged as his. She grimaced while looking down at her feet. "Wish we had time to let them dry, but it'll have to wait. I want to get Butterscotch home today."

He turned her in his arms and lowered his face until their lips were almost touching. "Any regrets?"

She rose and brushed her lips across his. "Only that my boots are still wet." She stared up into his eyes, a frown denting her forehead. "And you?"

His lips twisted into a teasing smile. "None. I happen to like soggy boots." He winked and kissed her for real. Not a brush across the lips. More of a lets-go-back-to-bed kind of kiss that rocked his soul and kind of scared him.

What was he doing? He was there to protect her, not to get into her pants.

It was a little late to be remembering his place in this relationship.

Hell, he'd have to tell Londyn's mother he couldn't work for her anymore because he was sleeping with her daughter. In turn, he'd have to tell Hank he fired himself from the job. Not a great start as a Brotherhood Protector.

He stared down at Londyn as she stroked her mare's nose and realized he didn't care. If losing his job was all that was keeping him from Londyn, it was a small price to pay.

Then, another thought occurred to him. What did he have to bring to the relationship? Londyn had only signed onto the film to save her ranch from foreclosure. If Nash didn't have a job, he had no way of helping her come up with the money to pay her way out of a financial hole.

"Just curious," he said. "You don't have to tell me, but how much money do you need to pay the back taxes and the mortgage on the ranch?"

"A lot," she said with a frown. "More than I've earned in my lifetime." She stared up at him. "Why?"

"Just curious." He didn't want to pry and make her uncomfortable, but if he could help, he would. While he'd been part of Delta Force, he'd deployed more than he was ever home. He hadn't had time to spend the money he'd made. When his bank account had gotten too full, he'd had a financial advisor invest it. He didn't really have an idea of how much he had squirreled away. Maybe enough to get Londyn's ranch out of debt…?

Her frown deepened. "Why do you want to know how much?"

He smiled. "I told you. I was just curious."

She continued to stare at him, her frown deepening.

"If you have some lame idea of cashing in your savings to pay off my debt, forget it." She crossed her arms over her chest. "I wouldn't let my mother help me, and she probably has a lot more money than you. If I can't find a way to save my ranch, I don't deserve to keep it. I have to find a way to do this." She poked a thumb at her chest. "Me. Not my mother. Not my lover. Me."

Nash held up his hands. "Sorry. I just was trying to think of a way to help."

"You are helping by protecting me from whoever is fucking with me. Keep me alive long enough to get through this gig, and all my problems will be solved. Do you understand?"

He popped a mock salute. "Yes, ma'am. Message received." She might not tell him what he wanted to know, but he was positive Swede could get that information.

A twinge of guilt tugged at Nash's gut. If she wanted him to know the amount, she would have told him. She didn't want anyone's help.

Still, he wanted to know to have an option in his back pocket should her plans fall through. The ranch meant a lot to her. It was her home.

Nash understood what it was to have a home. He'd grown up in a good one. He knew that if he had nowhere else to go, he could go home to his parents, no matter where they were, and they would happily take him in.

The exterior barn door opened, and a shaft of daylight spilled into the interior.

"Oh, good. You're awake." Dan Mitchell entered the barn and crossed to stand with Nash and Londyn. "Your mare appears to be recovering well."

Londyn nodded. "She does. We'll be leaving soon to take her back to my ranch in Montana. Thank you so much for all you did to help us find her and to put us up for the night."

Mitchell's mouth twisted into a wry grin. "You don't have to thank me. I felt bad that you slept in the barn all night. How was it? Did you get too cold?"

Londyn's cheeks turned a ruddy red.

"Not at all," Nash answered for her. "And we were able to keep tabs on Butterscotch. She even ate all the grain and hay your men left for her."

"Then she's definitely on the mend." Mitchell grinned. "You should have breakfast before you hit the road. Cookie made enough to feed the entire film crew, even though most of them left last night."

"Oh, we don't want to impose," Londyn said.

"If breakfast is half as good as the sandwiches Cookie left for us last night, we'd love to join you," Nash said. "And if he has more of the grapes he packed in with the sandwiches, we'd love to take some with us for a snack on our drive north."

Londyn snorted, her cheeks turning an even brighter shade of red.

Nash fought to keep from laughing. The grapes had been one of the best ideas he'd ever had to get them all hot and bothered after eating the delicious sandwiches. Not that they'd needed the grapes to reignite their passion. But it had been fun eating them off each other's bodies like Jell-O shots at a frat party.

"As a matter of fact, Cookie has a lot of those grapes left—and they need to be eaten before they go bad. I'll have him pack some for you to take with you. But for now, come on up to the house. Your cast-mates just came down for breakfast. I'm sure they'll want to hear all about your adventure in the rain last night."

"We'll be there in a minute," Nash assured him. "Could we get a little more grain for the mare? She's got an appetite this morning."

"Sure." Mitchell tipped his head toward a line of garbage cans. "The feed is kept in those cans. Help yourself to whatever she might like."

"We won't take much," Londyn said. "Just enough to satisfy, but not enough to have her getting sick on the trip."

"Sounds good," Mitchell said. "See you in a few minutes, and don't worry about cleaning the stalls. We'll take care of it."

"Thank you," Londyn said. "Will you at least let me pay you for boarding us for the night?"

Mitchell shook his head. "Not a chance. I might

decide to come visit you on your ranch someday. You can put me up in your barn."

Londyn smiled. "I'll do better than that. I have extra rooms in the house. I'll be sure to put fresh sheets on the bed."

"Gonna one-up me?" Mitchel shook his head with a smile tugging at the corners of his lips. He turned, chuckling. "Don't be too long, or the food will get cold."

Mitchell left the barn, and Londyn's gaze followed the other ranch owner. "There are good people in this world."

"Yes, there are." He glanced down at her. "Let's gather our things and get up to the ranch house for breakfast. I seemed to have worked up an appetite."

"For grapes?" Londyn shook her head, frowning, though her lips twitched on the corners. "I can't believe you asked for grapes. It's not like we can have a repeat of last night while driving to the ranch."

"I don't know," he said, giving her an assessing glance. "I love a challenge."

She backhanded him in the gut hard enough to get his attention but not hard enough to hurt. "Let's get going, grape nuts. I'd like to be on the road in less than an hour."

"Yes, ma'am," Nash said, chuckling. He leaned close. "The grapes have you salivating?"

"No, but Cookie's breakfast does." She shook her head and walked back into the stall with the sleeping bags. She lifted the one on the top, folded it over and zipped it together. Then she folded it in half and rolled it tightly, using the attached straps to secure it.

While she worked on one sleeping bag, he worked on the other. They gathered their wet clothing, the sleeping bags and the bag of clothing items Mitchell had offered that they wouldn't be using.

With their arms full, they checked Butterscotch once more, then headed to the house.

Cookie met them at the back door leading into the kitchen and held the door while they carried everything inside. "I just put the food out on the buffet in the dining room." He waved them toward the dining room. "Please. Help yourself. Do you want coffee, tea or juice?"

Nash entered the dining room, where a long table was set with plates, flatware and drink glasses.

Mitchell sat at the head of the table. Six men sat on either side. Julia Banes and Craig Ryland sat at the table, looking refreshed. Julia's hair was expertly coifed, and her make-up was subtle but beautiful. She smiled as Nash and Londyn entered the room. "Oh, there you two are. We're so glad you made it here, what with the storm and all."

"That's right," Craig said. "We were shocked to hear your horse ran away. Does that happen often?"

"It was a first," Londyn said. "Butterscotch has never displayed a reaction like that before."

"She's all right?" Julia asked.

Londyn nodded. "I'm taking her back to my ranch today."

"Anything I can do to help you?" Julia asked with a smile spread across her face.

"No, thank you," Londyn responded. "We can handle everything."

Nash loaded a plate full of food and set the plate on the table in the position beside Craig. He gave the man a nod and returned to stand with Londyn while she scooped fluffy, yellow scrambled eggs onto a plate and dropped two pieces of bacon on the side. She added a slice of bread before turning to the table. A slight frown pulled at her forehead as she claimed the seat beside Julia.

Nash snagged a slice of toast as an excuse for hanging out at the buffet for so long. He carried it to his plate across the table from where Londyn sat.

Craig's plate held the remains of scrambled eggs and half a slice of toast. He lifted his coffee mug to his lips and sipped gingerly. "We were so glad to hear you made it back last night and with your horse. What a nightmare being caught out in that storm."

"Thank you," Londyn said, not elaborating on the fact she nearly drowned.

"We heard from Haynes," Julia said. "They made it back to the trailers a few minutes before the storm hit their location."

"That's good," Nash said. "Driving in the deluge was...challenging." His gaze met Londyn's.

"Dan tells us you're heading back to your ranch with your horse." Her pretty eyebrows rose up her forehead. "Have you had enough fun playacting?"

Londyn stabbed at the eggs on her plate. "Not at all," she said. "But after what happened with my mare, she'll be better off recovering in familiar surroundings."

"Right," Julia said. "As I'm sure you'll be glad to be home as well."

"I will," Londyn said. "However short the stay."

"Is this the first time you've been away for this long?" Julia asked. "I mean, you appear to be more comfortable doing ranch things than acting."

"We were surprised when Haynes chose an unknown for the lead," Dan commented.

Londyn swallowed the piece of toast she'd been chewing. "No more surprised than when I got the part."

"I'm sure it didn't hurt that you're Dana Tyler's daughter," Julia said. "Not that anyone would know. You couldn't be more different in appearance from your mother."

"So, I'm told." Londyn smoothed jelly across her toast.

"Must be nice to eat carbs," Julia said. "I steer completely clear of them. Otherwise, I'd blow up like a blimp."

Londyn took a bite of her toast and closed her

eyes, moaning softly. After she swallowed, she said, "You're missing out."

Nash almost choked on his coffee. He liked that Londyn didn't rise to Julia's comments, and he liked that Londyn wasn't concerned about the carbs she consumed. Most likely, she burned it off, working her ranch. He understood the hard work required to raise cattle and horses and manage a large spread. That she was doing it by herself with just a couple of ranch hands amazed him and worried him about her health and safety.

"The weatherman predicts rain for the next couple of days," Craig said. "Perhaps Haynes will have us stand down until it clears."

"Which could give you more time at home," Julia said.

"That would be nice," Londyn murmured.

"If you like your ranch so much, why don't you stay?" Julia said.

Londyn sighed and turned to Mitchell. "How soon will we be able to stage the cattle drive?"

"It'll take a couple of days for the ground to dry enough to film the cattle drive," Mitchell said. "Unless your director wants muddy cows in the picture."

Londyn shook her head. "It's supposed to be a dusty summer scene. Besides, I'm sure you don't want to risk the safety of your herd, moving them on muddy turf."

Dan Mitchell nodded. "I am concerned. I'll speak with Haynes about the conditions."

"I suppose we'll be leaving today, as well," Julia said. "Though it was nice staying on a ranch. I can see why you love it so much," she said to Londyn. "I can't understand why you'd want to leave."

Londyn set her fork on her plate. "I have my reasons. Number one is that I have a job to do. I'll only be gone long enough to get my horse settled in. I'd appreciate it if you'd let Haynes know I'm only going long enough to get her settled in."

"I'm sure there's no hurry," Julia said. "I think the storm will have made a mess of our primary location as well as the cattle drive scene. We'll be up to our knees in mud for a few days until it dries."

Londyn met Nash's gaze across the table. "I'm ready when you are."

Nash nodded, aware of the tension between Londyn and Julia. The other actress had a way of getting under even his skin—and her comments weren't directed at him. The tightness around Londyn's mouth was a clear indication Julia's comments were hitting nerves. He glanced at Mitchell. "We'll be leaving within the hour. Thank you for your hospitality."

Mitchell snorted. "Next time, let me treat you to a real bed."

Nash wanted to tell the ranch owner the night in the barn had been perfect. But then it might give the people at the table a hint as to why it had been so perfect. He wasn't the kind of guy to kiss and tell. If he knew anything about Londyn, her privacy was important to her, too.

He stood and rounded the table to hold Londyn's chair as she rose to her feet. They gathered their plates and cups.

"Don't worry about the dishes; we'll take care of them," Mitchell said. "You need to get your mare ready for the trip."

"Thanks, but we can at least carry our things into the kitchen." Nash followed Londyn into the kitchen.

Cookie stood before a huge sink with his arms up to his elbows in soapy water. When they set their plates and cups beside him, he gave them a grateful grin. "Thanks. Did you get enough to eat?"

Londyn touched his shoulder. "More than enough. Thank you for making such a tasty breakfast."

"Yes," Nash said. "Better than any chow hall food I've had."

Cookie laughed. "Funny you should say that. I learned to cook in a Navy chow hall."

"Then the Navy had far superior food than the Army." Nash clapped a hand on the older man's shoulder. "Thank you for your service."

Cookie rinsed the soap off his hands and dried them on a towel. He stuck out his clean hand. "And thank you for your service."

Nash gripped it with a firm handshake. When he let go, he turned, placed a hand on the small of Londyn's back and escorted her out the kitchen door.

"Wait just a minute," Cookie called out.

Nash and Londyn turned back into the kitchen.

Cookie ducked into a pantry and emerged with two bright red apples and a bag of grapes. He gave them a crooked grin. "Mitch said you wanted some grapes to snack on while you're traveling. The apples are for your horse."

When Londyn's face flushed red, Nash fought the urge to laugh out loud. He took the offerings from the cook, holding onto the bag of grapes and handing the apples to Londyn. "Thank you for your kindness. We'll definitely enjoy the grapes."

"Yes, thanks. Butterscotch loves apples," Londyn said and spun toward the exit.

Nash followed Londyn through the door and out onto the wraparound porch.

Londyn refused to look at him as she crossed the porch to the stairs. "We used to have a cook at the ranch," she said, clearly changing the subjects. "When he retired and moved to Florida to be closer to his children, Gramps and I shared the responsibility to keep our ranch hands fed."

"It's like I said," Nash grinned. "Food is fuel."

"For the body as well as the soul." She laughed softly, her eyes getting glassy with moisture. "Gramps always said that. His repertoire in the kitchen wasn't vast, but it was hearty and always felt like home. He worked as hard in the kitchen as he did outside. After our cook left, he never expected me to take over the cooking as a woman's duty. I did my share, though. We both washed dishes, taking turns over who would wash and who would dry."

"I think I would've liked your grandfather," Nash said as they descended the steps and crossed to the barn. "You never talk about your grandmother. If it's a sore subject, you don't have to answer."

"Oh, it's not a sore subject at all. She died when my mother was a young teen. I never met her. My grandfather didn't talk about her. I think he loved her so much that, when she died, he had a hard time getting over it. I've seen pictures of her when she was younger. My mother looked just like her."

"That had to be hard for your grandfather. He had to see his wife in your mother's face."

Londyn nodded. "An everyday reminder of the woman he'd lost. It probably led to the rift between them. Once she left the ranch, she didn't come back until Gramps' funeral."

Nash opened the barn door and held it for Londyn to enter.

"Do you and your mother get along?" Nash asked.

"Of course. Once she let me go live at the ranch, we got along better than ever. I visited her in LA during the holidays and spoke with her on the phone at least once a week. I love her." Londyn grimaced. "I just can't live her lifestyle. Which I'm sure is a great disappointment to her."

Londyn stopped in front of Butterscotch's stall. The mare whinnied and stuck her head over the door.

"Hey, sweet girl." Londyn held out an apple.

The mare took the fruit and crunched it between her teeth while Londyn rubbed her nose. "Are you ready to go home?"

Having finished the apple, the mare tossed her head as if saying *yes*. Then she nuzzled Londyn's empty hand, looking for the other apple she had hidden behind her back.

Londyn laughed and gave the mare the other apple. "You're too smart for your own good."

While the mare ate the second apple, Nash opened the stall door. He and Londyn entered and walked around the animal, looking for any signs of trauma they might have missed the night before.

Londyn ran her hand over the mare's legs one at a time and lifted each foot to inspect her hooves. "She has some scratches on her legs, but nothing major for having taken off like a bat out of hell. She's lucky. As am I." Londyn smiled up at Nash. "Thanks again for saving both of us."

"Just doing my job as a protector," he said, knowing it was more than that.

"Well then, thanks for doing your job." She gripped the lead. "Let's get her loaded up. I'd like to get to the ranch with as much daylight left in the day as possible so that I can check things out."

He nodded and held the stall door open.

Londyn led the buckskin out of the stall and out of the barn.

Nash moved ahead of Londyn to open the doors to the barn and then to the horse trailer.

At first, Butterscotch balked at the trailer. After Londyn worked with her for the next few minutes, the mare walked up into the trailer with no problem.

Once the horse was loaded and the back door to the trailer closed and latched, Nash opened the passenger seat door for Londyn.

She frowned up at him. "I can drive."

"I know you can," he said. "But I'd like to do the honors if you would be all right with it."

Her eyes narrowed as she studied him. "I suppose." She climbed up into the truck.

Nash stepped up on the running board and secured her seatbelt around her hips.

"I can—" she started.

"—do it yourself." He grinned down at her, brushed his lips across her forehead and smiled. "I know. Humor me. I need to feel useful."

Her lips twitched. "Okay." She captured his face between her palms and brushed her lips across his. "But only because I'm tired and want to sleep on the way. I'm sure there will be work to do once we arrive at LJ Ranch."

He cupped the back of her neck and kissed her properly. "I'm sure you'll be fully occupied once we get you home. I'm just glad to be of assistance."

Her lips twisted into a wry smile. "You know that you're more than useful."

"I hope so." He dropped to the ground, closed her door and rounded the truck to the driver's side, slipping into the seat, damp boots and all. "How far is it to your place?"

"About four hours, as long as it doesn't rain," she said.

He nodded, buckled his seatbelt and started the engine.

Before he could shift into gear, Julia Banes ran out of the house and hurried over to Nash's side of the truck.

Nash lowered his window. "Everything all right?"

Julia laughed. "Yes, of course. I just wanted to let Londyn know I heard from Director Haynes. He put us on hiatus for at least the next three days while the sets dry. No need to hurry back."

Londyn leaned forward to stare at the other actor. "I can be back within four hours, should they need me sooner. All he has to do is text or call."

"I'll let him know," Julia said. "Enjoy your time at home." She backed away from the truck and trailer and waved as Nash drove out of the barnyard and onto the gravel road leading off the ranch.

Nash glanced in the side mirror, looking back at the barn and the ranch house.

Craig Ryland came out of the house and joined Julia as she stood watching the truck and trailer drive away from Mitchell's place.

They'd be heading back to the original location soon, which meant Londyn had very little time to reposition.

"What do you know about Julia Banes and Craig Ryland?" Nash asked.

Londyn leaned her head back against the headrest. "Not much. Why?"

"Does one or more of the cast or crew have any reason to want to see you fail in your role as Lana?" he asked.

Londyn's brow dipped low. "I don't know. I haven't engaged in the Hollywood politics or drama." She turned her head toward Nash. "Why do you ask?"

"Were you targeted before you came to work on the set or after?"

Her lips pressed together. "After."

"Was anyone upset that you got the part of Lana?" Nash asked. "Upset enough to want to kill you?"

Londyn's brow twisted. "I never thought about it. I was focused on earning the money I needed to save the ranch. Besides, who would want to kill me for a part in a movie?"

Nash's eyebrows rose up his forehead. "Probably a hundred starving artists in LA."

Londyn's eyes narrowed. "Don't you think murder is taking it a bit far?"

Nash laughed. "Yes. Absolutely. But how many actors audition for years without actually landing a part in a potential blockbuster movie?"

Londyn shrugged. "I don't know."

Nash snorted. "You landed a role on your first audition."

Londyn blinked up at him. "Is that unusual?"

"Yeah." Nash shot a glance her way before returning his attention to the gravel road leading off the ranch. "Many would say you didn't pay your dues."

"I don't even like acting," Londyn said.

"It doesn't matter if you like acting or not. You got the part."

She pinched the bridge of her nose. "I would never have attempted acting if I didn't need the money so badly."

Nash nodded. "When we get to a location with better cell phone reception, I need to touch base with Swede and see what he's learned from his background check of all the cast and crew members."

Londyn leaned her head back again and closed her eyes. "I can't imagine anyone wanting my part badly enough to want to kill me to have it. It's ridiculous—and far too obvious."

"Jealousy and greed don't always come along with clear thinking," Nash noted.

"If someone wants to kill me for a chance at the lead female character's part in this movie, don't you think the authorities would start their investigation with all the ladies who auditioned and didn't get the part?"

"That's what I would do," Nash said.

"Not only would she have to want to kill me, but she'd also have to have the skills necessary to work with plastic explosives. She'd also need the ability to handle a horse. And she'd have to have dark hair, dark skin and look like a Native American. That had was the number one requirement Haynes insisted on."

"Don't you think that with enough makeup and the right wig, anyone could pass as Native American?" Nash asked.

"Not necessarily," Londyn said. "It's not just about the makeup and hair. Facial structure has a lot to do with Haynes's choice of actor to play the part. He needed my character to have a certain look, determination and the ability to kick ass, should the need arise."

Nash grinned. "He chose wisely with you."

She nodded. "Fortunately, others won't have the opportunity to be Lana. Haynes is stuck with me until it's a wrap. I need the money,"

Nash nodded. "If, as you said, she really has her finger on the pulse of Hollywood, we need to talk to your mother sooner rather than later."

Londyn sighed and closed her eyes. "When we get to the ranch, I'll call her. For now, I really want to take a nap. I didn't get much sleep last night."

Nash's lips curled up in a grin. "Me, either."

Though Londyn's eyes remained closed, her mouth curved in a smile. "What did you do with those grapes Cookie gave you?"

He chuckled. "I'm saving those for when we get to LJ Ranch. I have plans for those grapes."

Her eyelids opened for a brief moment as she cast a glance his way. "Are you going to share them?"

His gaze met hers briefly. "Absolutely."

Londyn closed her eyes again and leaned her head against the headrest of her seat. "Then I really do need a nap." She covered her mouth as she yawned. "Wake me if you need me to drive."

"Sleep," Nash said. "I've got this."

"You didn't get any more sleep than I did last night."

"I can get by on a lot less sleep than the average man," he said.

"Because you're not an average man," Londyn said softly.

"I'll take that as a compliment."

"Do that," she said. "And wake me when we get there."

True to her word, Londyn leaned her head against the door. She was out in under two minutes.

Nash spent the next few hours studying her face,

committing thick eyelashes, exotic skin tone and proud angles to memory. She was a beautiful woman with a drive and determination he hadn't witnessed in many other women.

After memorizing every line and contour of her face and remembering the sexy curves of her body now encased in sweats, Nash came to a startling conclusion.

He liked her.

Really liked her.

If he wasn't careful, he could fall in love with this woman.

The air left his lungs.

He turned his full attention back to the road, where it should be—not on the woman sleeping peacefully beside him. To keep her safe, he needed complete focus.

His gaze slipped to Londyn as if it had a mind of its own.

CHAPTER 13

"HEY, SWEETHEART," a deep voice said as if from the end of a long tunnel. "Wake up."

A hand on Londyn's shoulder shook her gently.

She blinked her eyes open and stared out through the front windshield of her truck at the house that had been her home for the past twenty-one years. Her heart swelled with joy.

Home.

As quickly as the joy filled her, it vanished. Gramps wouldn't come out on the porch to greet her ever again. He wouldn't be there to give her his gruff hugs or sage advice.

A big black Ford F-250 pickup was parked beside them.

"Does the truck belong to one of your ranch hands?" Nash asked.

Londyn had to think about it for a second before

she remembered. "No. It belongs to Ben Standing Bear."

Nash frowned. "Did you let him know that we were coming?"

Londyn sat up straight and pushed her hair out of her face. "No, I didn't." She reached for the door handle and pushed it open. "He's probably just here checking things out. He promised to look out for things while I was gone." She slid out of the truck and closed the door.

Nash dropped down from the truck and met her at the front. Together, they walked up the front porch steps.

Voices sounded inside the house. Londyn frowned. One of those voices was female. A voice she knew.

She grabbed the door handle and twisted. It was not locked. She pushed it inward and stepped inside.

Ben Standing Bear stood with his back to her, talking to someone. "You have to tell her, or I will."

When the door hinge creaked, Ben turned, his dark eyebrows forming a V over his nose.

Londyn could see the woman he was talking to, and she gasped. "Mother?"

"Londyn, darling." Dana Tyler hurried forward to grasp Londyn's hands. "I'm so glad you've arrived."

"Why are you here?" Londyn looked from her mother to Ben Standing Bear. "You two know each other?"

Dana Tyler's face blushed a pretty pink. "Yes, we do. We grew up together."

Ben had moved to stand by the window, looking out. "Did you bring your mare back?" Londyn shifted her gaze to the man standing by the window. "Yes, I did. She had some kind of psychotic episode and took off yesterday. It was the strangest thing I've ever seen her do. When we finally found her, she was exhausted. I'm unsure what got into her, but the veterinarian took a blood sample and sent it off for testing. In the meantime, I knew she'd be better off in familiar surroundings. So, we brought her home."

"Have you unloaded her yet?" Ben asked.

"No," Londyn said. "We just got here."

"I'll take care of her." Ben glanced toward her mother. "I'm sure you two ladies have things to talk about." He stepped out the front door.

"If you don't need me for now, I'll help him." Nash hesitated.

Londyn lifted her chin. "I'll be fine."

Nash hurried after Ben.

Once the two men were out of the house, Londyn met her mother's gaze. "You never come to the ranch. What's wrong?"

Her mother squeezed her hands and let go. "I had a small charter plane fly me into your film location in Yellowstone. When I asked where you were, Director Haynes said you'd quit."

"What?" Londyn stared at her mother as if she'd lost her mind. "I did no such thing."

"Well, Haynes is convinced you did." Her mother pushed her thick blond hair back from her forehead. "Why would he think you had quit if you had not?"

"I don't know." Londyn shook her head. "I never said I quit. Director Haynes wasn't there this morning when I left the T-Bar-M Ranch. Since cell phone reception is less than optimal, I asked Craig to let him know that I'd be gone for at least a day and to let me know when filming resumes. I'd get back."

"That's not what Craig told me," her mother said. "He said that you'd had enough and were headed home to stay."

Londyn continued to shake her head. "He's lying."

Her mother's lips pressed together. "I trust Craig. He's a good guy. I gave him his start in the industry. I got him this part. The man owes me."

"I'm telling you he's lying." Londyn paced across the living room and back.

"He has no reason to lie," her mother said. "Maybe because you left, he thinks you quit…?"

Londyn spun to face her mother. "I specifically told him I was only taking my horse back home and that I would be available as soon as they were ready to resume filming. That's the message I asked him to pass on to Haynes."

Dana Tyler lifted her chin and squared her shoulders. "Arguing isn't fixing the problem. They'll resume filming tomorrow at the Yellowstone location. You need to be there to explain to director Haynes that you did not quit. He was given incorrect information. In fact, I can have you flown back tonight in the plane that I chartered."

Londyn held her mother's gaze. "I'm going to take a couple of hours to check how things have been going on the ranch. If you want to fly me back, you can do that tomorrow morning." When her mother opened her mouth to argue, Londyn shut her down with a hard stare. "I'm not being unreasonable. Yesterday's storm was pretty rough."

Dana Tyler's lips pressed into a thin line, creating a dark streak of red across her face. Finally, she nodded. "Very well. I'll have my pilot on standby. We'll leave before dawn." Her face softened. "For the record, I'm glad you're okay."

"Thank you," Londyn said. "Now, if you'll excuse me, I'm going to shower and change into some of my own clothes and dry boots. Then I'm going to get outside and see what's been happening while I've been gone." Londyn headed for the staircase.

Her mother touched her arm. "Londyn, there's something I need to tell you."

Londyn stared down the hand on her arm. "Mother, I'm tired. In the past few days, someone has tried to kill me, *I* almost killed someone, and I nearly drowned trying to rescue my horse. Can whatever you have to tell me wait until after I have a shower, dress in warm, clean clothes and boots that don't squish when I walk?"

Her mother, who always knew everything and everyone and never hesitated, especially on big decisions, chewed on her bottom lip for a couple of seconds. Then, she nodded. "Get that shower. And the change of clothes." Her mother smiled. "And definitely put on dry boots. But Londyn, we need to talk. I've put things off for far too long."

Londyn gave her a curt nod and climbed the stairs to the room that had been hers since she'd been six years old and first came to live with her grandfather. Having been away for several weeks, she stood in the doorway and looked at it with a fresh perspective.

The room hadn't changed much in all the years. A white iron bed stood in the center. It had been her mother's when she'd been growing up and then Londyn's. Londyn's grandmother had made the faded quilt draped over the mattress. She'd had many opportunities to replace that quilt with a more modern comforter, but she hadn't had the heart to do it. It was the one connection to her mother and her grandmother that she had refused to sever.

She turned her head to glance at the end of the hallway to the half-opened door into her grandfather's room. A lump formed in her throat, and tears spilled down her cheeks.

After the trauma of the day before, her emotions were raw. What she needed was a hug.

Her thoughts went to Nash. He'd made love to her last night, awakening her body to delights she hadn't experienced before. Then he'd held her in his arms, his muscular frame cocooning her in warmth and strength. For the first time since Gramps had died, she hadn't felt so alone.

She grabbed underwear, jeans and a blouse and ducked into the bathroom across the hall from her room. If she'd learned one thing from her grandfather's death, it was to keep moving. If you were busy, you didn't have time to feel sorry for yourself.

Londyn made quick work of her shower, scrubbing the creek water from her hair and applying a healthy dose of conditioner to help smooth the tangles. Once clean, she turned off the water and grabbed a towel. She dried her body and wrapped her hair in the towel to help absorb the majority of the moisture.

Anxious to get outside, Londyn dressed quickly in worn blue jeans, a chambray shirt and her work boots. She ran a brush through her hair, wishing Nash was there to ease the tangles free. He'd been so gentle and sexy.

Clean and tangle-free, she left the bathroom and hurried down the stairs and out the back door, half-walking, half-running toward the barn.

She found Nash standing outside the barn with a garden hose, spraying the creek water and mud off the buckskin mare.

Nash had stripped off his shirt and hung it over a fence rail. His broad chest was nicely tanned with a smattering of man-curls begging her to run her finger across them. Like she had the night before. The scars on his face and across his torso only added to his appeal.

Londyn's pulse pounded through her veins, and her mouth went dry.

He turned off the water and coiled the hose on a hanger affixed to the side of the barn. "You're just in time. I could use some towels. Are there some in the barn?"

Londyn nodded. "In the tack room. I'll get them." To keep from openly drooling over him, she ducked into the barn and into the tack room. She gathered several towels and held them against her chest, willing her heart to slow to a normal pace.

When she had her breathing under control, she emerged from the barn and handed him a towel.

Without meeting his gaze, she dove into the task of drying Butterscotch. "Where did Ben go?" she asked.

"He said he had work to do on his place," Nash said as he rubbed a towel across the mare's back. "The ranch hands are mending a fence in your south pasture. A tree blew over onto it. They should be done soon. Ben will be back later this evening."

Londyn gave Nash a tired smile. "Thanks."

"What are your plans for the day?" Nash asked.

"I want to ride the fences, check the animals and get a feeling for how everything is faring without me." She raised her eyebrows. "Do you want to come?"

He nodded. "I do. I'd like to get a shower first."

"Of course," Londyn said. "I bet I can find something for you to wear. My grandfather was a big man, much like you." She glanced down at his feet. "He might even have a pair of boots that will fit."

"I'd love that," Nash said. "I'm to the point I'd rather go barefoot than wear these boots another minute."

"Let's finish up with Butterscotch. She doesn't need to be confined to a stall. When she's done eating, we can release her into the pasture."

"I'd like to contact Swede and see if he came up with any hits on the names of the cast and crew."

"If you can't get enough reception for your cell phone, you can use the landline in the kitchen."

"Thanks," Nash said. "Ben fed Butterscotch. She's ready for the pasture."

"Good," Londyn rubbed her hand along the animal's neck. She hooked her fingers through the halter. "Ready to go hang out with the gang?"

Nash held the barn door open for Londyn and Butterscotch and walked with them to a gate. He opened the gate.

Londyn walked through with Butterscotch. "You're on vacation now," she said, rubbing the horse's nose. "Enjoy it while it lasts. I'll see you in a few weeks."

Butterscotch trotted off to join the other horses on the far end of the pasture.

Londyn's gaze followed her all the way. "She wasn't the same horse yesterday when she ran off."

"No, she wasn't. But she seems back to normal now and happy to be home." Nash leaned on the fence rail, staring out at the animals in the pasture. "Are you going to ride a different horse around the property?"

"I was thinking more along the lines of taking four-wheelers," Londyn said.

"I'm game either way. Give me ten minutes for that shower, and I'll be ready."

They walked back to the house together. Londyn led him through the back door and up the stairs to the bathroom. "There are towels in the cabinet and shampoo in the shower. I'll be back with clothes that might fit you."

Nash was already unzipping his jeans when Londyn turned to leave. She was tempted to stay and help him. But there was a lot she wanted to do and see before she headed back to Yellowstone.

The only clothes Londyn could think of that would fit Nash were her grandfather's clothes. Gramps had been a big man, standing over six feet tall with broad shoulders and thick muscular arms. She hadn't been back in his room since the funeral when she'd had to pick his best Sunday suit for the viewing.

With a deep breath, Londyn squared her shoulders and marched down the hall and into her grandfather's bedroom. It still smelled like him, and that smell almost brought her to her knees. As she fought back tears, she crossed to his closet, opened the doors and thumbed through the hangers full of neatly pressed denim jeans. The jeans were well-worn and faded. Some had rips that had been patched, and others had frayed hems. But they were her grandfather's, and she hadn't had the heart to donate them to a local shelter. She wiped away a tear that had trickled out of the corner of her eye and grabbed a hanger with a pair of blue jeans on it.

"My father wasn't always gruff and seemingly unfeeling."

Londyn spun toward the voice.

Dana Tyler stood near the four-poster bed her father had slept in for most of his life. "He changed when my mother died. It was like the light went out of him. Sadly, I looked so much like my mother that he couldn't even look at me. He was heartbroken. But so was I. I needed him, and he wasn't there for me. I acted out for attention, and all it got me was the wrong kind of attention. It seemed like I was always crossways with my father through my teen years. I didn't have my mother to talk to. I didn't have many close friends at school. Just my boyfriend."

"Is that why you left home and never came back?" Londyn asked. "All because you butted heads with Gramps once too often?" Londyn's brow puckered as she stared at her mother. "Gramps was a good man. He didn't always know how to show his love, but he did love me, and I know he loved you, too. It always hurt to know that the two people I cared about most never made the effort to reconcile. You were both so stubborn." Tears flowed down Londyn's cheeks. "It broke his heart when he lost Grandma. It broke all over again when he lost you. It took him a long time to open his heart to me, but he did." She brushed the tears from her cheeks. "And I loved him very much, and I miss him every single day. He was the father I never had."

Her mother stared out at the fields and the mountains beyond. "I left because the man I fell in love with told me he didn't love me anymore. I'd wrapped all my hopes and dreams around him. When he broke my heart, I had to leave. I couldn't be in the same town or the same state with him without being reminded of everything I'd lost." She turned to face Londyn, tears streaming down her face. "You see, my father disapproved of my boyfriend. In fact, he told my boyfriend to leave me alone because he couldn't provide the kind of life I deserved." She turned back toward the window. "Granted, we were just kids, having just graduated high school with no firm plans for our future." She snorted. "We were convinced love would find a way. We didn't care that we were dirt poor. We both knew the value of hard work and were convinced a life together was what we wanted."

"But you said your boyfriend broke up with you," Londyn said.

Her mother nodded. "My father got to him. After they had a little discussion, my boyfriend didn't think he was good enough for me and thought I would be better off without him. So, he staged the breakup, even though he really still loved me. He said awful things to make me hate him. I was hurting so bad that when my father cornered me and told me it was all for the best, I blew up. I said things that I'd been bottling up for years after Mom's death. I packed my bags and left, promising never to return. It wasn't until I got to LA that I realized I was pregnant."

"With me." Londyn's whole world seemed to shift. "So, your one-night stand at the bar wasn't my father, was it?"

Her mother shook her head.

"In fact, there wasn't a one-night stand at the bar." Londyn's teeth ground together.

"No," her mother admitted.

"You've known who my father is all my life." Londyn said that as a statement not a question.

"Yes." Dana Tyler's beautiful face was drawn, making her look older than her forty-five years.

Londyn slung the jeans over her shoulder and

reached blindly into the closet for a button-down shirt.

She grabbed for a pair of her grandfather's work boots and went to his dresser where she fished out a pair of socks.

"Londyn, talk to me." Her mother touched her arm.

She glared at her mother. "That might not be a good idea right now. I'm so mad, I'm literally seeing red." She left the room and stomped down the hall to the bathroom. The door was unlocked. Londyn pushed it open, dropped her armload of clothing onto the floor and closed the door again softly.

Her mother followed her down the hall.

Londyn couldn't face her at that moment. She needed to get outside and breathe fresh air that wasn't polluted by the lies that have been fed to her all her life.

She headed for the stairs and ran down them like the hounds of hell were snapping at her heels.

Her mother hurried after her, stopping at the top of the stairs. "Londyn, you need to know."

I need to know now? Is she serious?

I needed to know from the day I was born.

Londyn didn't stop running. She pushed through the back door and ran out onto the porch drawing in deep ragged breaths. It wasn't enough. She ran to the barn and rushed in without looking where she was going.

She ran into Ben Standing Bear, who caught her arms and held her steady. The tears she'd held in check burst free. Ben looked down at her, his brow furrowed and concern written across his kind face. "She told you." His words echoed through her mind.

Londyn looked up at the man, and the pieces of her life fell into place. Anger surged inside, burning hot and fast.

She pushed both hands against Ben's chest, forcing him to release his hold on her arms. She stepped back and glared at the man. "It's you. It's been you all along. You lived right next door to us, and you never said anything. You never once tried to be a part of my life."

"I didn't know." He raised his chin. "I suspected it, but I didn't *know* until your grandfather told you to come to me for help. If I had known you were my daughter, I would've done everything in my power to be there for you."

"Well, you weren't. And my mother was too busy living the life of a celebrity in LA. I was a big winner in the lottery of parents." She pushed past him and marched to the back of the barn where they kept the four-wheelers. She sat on the first one she came to and tried to start it. The engine wouldn't turn over. Dead battery.

She flung herself onto the one beside it. This one started, the engine roaring to life. Londyn shifted into the gear and twisted the handle, sending the ATV leaping forward.

Ben stepped aside as she blasted past him and out into the barnyard.

Nash was half-way across the yard when Londyn blew past him and angled toward another gate.

"Londyn, wait," Nash called out.

She only stopped long enough to dismount and open the gate. Then she climbed back onto the ATV and drove through the gate, leaving it open.

If Nash wanted to go with her, he'd have to hurry to catch up. If he didn't catch up, it might be for the best. Londyn was angry and had a lot to digest.

Ben Standing Bear was her father. Her mother and her grandfather had kept that secret all this time.

Londyn raced across the pasture, heading toward the south fence where her ranch hands were working. She didn't really want to talk to anyone. Not after learning her family had lied to her for her entire life. What family does that to the people they supposedly love?

She gave the ATV all the power, racing across the grasslands. The wind in her face and the power of the engine vibrating beneath her helped soothe the anger. When she climbed up a rise, she slowed to a stop. This was the place she loved most. The hills rising from the prairie grass gave her the best view of the grassland, with the Crazy Mountains in the background.

The ATV engine rumbled beneath her loud enough that she didn't hear the approach of another four-wheeler until it was almost on her.

She turned to find Nash driving his vehicle up to park beside hers. For the longest time, he didn't say anything; he simply reached out a hand.

Londyn took the hand and held on to it. "I don't know who to trust anymore," she whispered.

He didn't respond. She was glad he didn't. Most men she'd met always wanted to fix problems.

Londyn didn't need him to fix the problem. She just needed him to be there. To hold her hand and maybe hold the rest of her.

"What are you going to do?" Nash asked softly.

She snorted. "I'm going to check my employees, the fences and the livestock. Then I'm going back to Yellowstone to finish what I started."

"And your mother and father?"

Londyn stared at rolling hills and grassland. It never seemed to change. Everything else in her life had changed completely. "If you're asking whether or not I'll forgive them... The answer is probably. Never in my wildest dreams did I expect to meet my biological father." She sighed. "When Gramps died, I felt so alone. It made me realize that no matter how angry I get with my mother, I don't want to lose her. She's all the family I have left. Even if we don't live compatible lifestyles, she's still my mother."

"And now that you know who your father is..." Nash prompted.

Londyn shook her head in silence. "All the years we could have shared..." She met his gaze. "All the years people didn't believe I was Dana Tyler's daughter because I don't look anything like my mother..." She laughed without humor. "I look like Ben."

Nash nodded. "So, what now?"

She drew in a breath and let it out slowly. "I make my rounds, check things out and head back to Yellowstone in the morning. I want to know why Craig Ryland told the director I quit."

CHAPTER 14

Nash rode alongside Londyn, checking the entire perimeter of the LJ Ranch. She'd met with the ranch hands and listened as they'd caught her up on what they'd been doing since she'd been gone. They'd also shared their plans for the next month.

Ben Standing Bear had taken his promise to help keep an eye on her place seriously and had the ranch hands working on projects to shore up damaged fences and gates. He'd purchased fencing supplies out of his own pocket.

Londyn hadn't been happy about that. When she'd gotten back to the house, she'd told her mother she'd pay Ben back as soon as she received her first paycheck. Other than that bit of information, she was still giving her mother the cold shoulder.

Nash figured she'd come around soon enough.

She had the right to be angry. Her mother had lied to her about her father.

That evening, Ben joined them for dinner, coming early enough to throw steaks and baked potatoes on the grill.

Nash helped Londyn chop vegetables for a salad. The ranch hands joined them, and they all sat at the big table in the kitchen. Having the ranch hands in the room helped keep the mood light. They told stories of crazy things that happened in the weeks since Londyn had been gone

Despite the ranch hands' antics and stories, by the end of the meal, Londyn's body was strung tighter than a compound bow.

When the ranch hands insisted on doing the dishes, Nash helped Londyn carry plates into the kitchen, then took her hand and led her out onto the porch. The sun had set, and the sky was sprinkled with so many glittering stars that they didn't need the porch light to see.

Nash walked with Londyn around the house and down to the barn, where they leaned on the top rail of the fence and watched the horses in the field beyond.

"I feel like everything has changed," Londyn whispered. "And yet, most things have stayed the same. I still need to finish this acting contract. The bank still wants back mortgage payments, and the state is sending notices demanding payment of back taxes." Her lips twisted into a sad smile.

"Then what has changed?" Nash asked, wanting her to articulate what was going on inside.

"I don't know if I can ever trust my mother to tell me the truth, for one. She lied to me all my life. Why couldn't she just tell me who my father was?"

"Like you," her mother said from behind her, "I didn't want to rely on anyone else to help raise my child. You have to understand. Ben said terrible things to me. He told me he'd never loved me and only hung around because I was pretty. He said he was tired of my clinginess and was ready to move on and date other girls."

Ben Standing Bear appeared behind Londyn's mother. "I said some heinous things to your mother. I didn't believe any of them, but I needed *her* to believe them. Your grandfather had convinced me that I wasn't good enough for his daughter, that I would hold her back from exploring her greatest potential."

Dana slipped her hand through the crook of Ben's elbow. "The truth was that I wasn't good enough for Ben. I should've seen through his ruse."

"Dana's father pointed out that we were just two young people with no job prospects," Ben said, his gaze going to the stars in the sky. "I didn't have a college degree or own land I could work to make money. I'd need to provide for a wife and any children that might come along." He laughed. "I admit, he painted a pretty bleak picture of life as an unemployed Native American. He said the best thing I could do was break it off with his daughter. I should let her go to college, get her education, and establish herself in a career. I could also use that time to improve my situation. Then, if she came back to me, he'd bless our union. Only then would she be more of an asset than a liability."

Londyn's mother's lips pursed into a tight line. "That was my father. More concerned about profitability than his only daughter's world falling apart around her ears."

"The point is," Ben faced Dana and took her hand, "your father was right. Had we married straight out of high school, you wouldn't have had the opportunity to audition for parts in LA."

"I wasn't even interested in acting," Dana said, "until I had to do something to support my kid." She glanced toward Londyn. "I didn't tell Ben about his daughter because he'd made it clear he didn't want anything to do with me. That cut so deep. I didn't want him to feel obligated to support her. I'd severed ties with my father and was alone in LA. I had to figure it out on my own."

Ben looked down into Dana's eyes. "I shouldn't have been so horrible to you. If I had gone with our original plan, we'd have been married before Londyn was born."

Her mother arched an eyebrow. "And you might

not have gone to college and become a hot shot financial planner and made enough money to buy the property next to my father's and so much more."

He snorted. "I admit I wanted to prove him wrong. I wanted to make it big enough that I deserved you. I even went to LA after I bought the ranch."

Londyn's mother gazed up into Ben's eyes. "You did? Why did I not know this?"

He grimaced. "I had some ridiculous idea that I could win you back if I just told you the truth and showed you that I could provide for a family." Ben sighed.

She stared into his eyes. "I didn't know."

"I saw you from a distance at the red-carpet premiere of the movie that shot you to stardom. You'd made it. I realized then that I didn't have a chance. Your father was right. You were so much better off without me. So, I got on the plane, came back home and worked my ranch."

"You never married," Dana said.

He shook his head. "The only girl I ever wanted to marry was way out of my league." He faced Londyn. "So, you see, neither of us intentionally deprived you of the family you deserved."

Londyn sighed. "Could you at least let me be mad for a few more days? It doesn't make up for the twenty-seven years I missed out on having a father around who could've taken me to the father-daughter dances and taught me to throw a baseball." She shook her head. "I think, in his own gruff way, Gramps tried to make up for splitting you two up by taking me in and teaching me all the things a father would've taught me."

"I think he was also making up for checking out of my life after my mother died," Dana said. "He couldn't look at me because I looked like Mom."

"And that's why he was more willing to take me in," Londyn said. "I don't look anything like my mother or grandmother." She met Ben's gaze. "I look like my father." Her brow twisted. "That's going to take some getting used to. Don't take offense if I continue to call you Ben."

Ben held up a hand. "I won't take offense if you won't take offense if I don't call you my little girl."

Londyn laughed. "I won't."

Her mother gave her a hopeful look. "So, are we okay? You aren't going to hate me forever? I realized far too late that hate hurts you more than the person you profess to hate." She pulled Londyn into her arms. "I'm sorry I didn't tell you sooner."

"I might forgive you...someday. Just not today." Londyn wrapped her arms around her mother and held her for a long moment, her eyes dangerously moist. "I wish Gramps could've been here for this love fest." She chuckled. "He would've felt awkward as hell, but I think he would've liked to make things right. Otherwise, why would he have sent me to Ben upon his death?"

"Guilty conscience," Dana said. "It probably helped him lighten the burden in his heart." She leaned into Ben. "I guess the next big question is where to from here?"

Ben slipped an arm around her waist and pulled her close. "For now, it's enough to take it one day at a time."

"As much as I enjoy the night sky and cool temperatures, I'll leave you two to get reacquainted," Londyn said. "I have to get up early tomorrow to fly down to Yellowstone and salvage what's left of my debut and finale in the film industry. I still need the money." She gave her mother a tight smile. "Does your offer to fly me down there still stand?"

Her mother nodded. "It does. In anticipation of your reunion with the director, I gave the pilot the warning order earlier this evening. He'll be ready and waiting for you and Nash before dawn."

"Then I'm going to get some rest," Londyn said.

Her mother held up a hand. "One other thing on the road to transparency..."

Nash tensed along with Londyn as the older woman grinned. "It's okay. I just thought you'd like to know why I named you Londyn." She smiled.

"As a matter of fact, I am curious," Londyn cocked an eyebrow. "Why did you name me Londyn? And then spell it wrong?"

Dana looked up into Ben's gaze. "Do you remember what you wrote in my yearbook?"

Ben's brow dipped. "We were planning our honeymoon, though we didn't have the money to take one."

"We were going to London." She smiled weakly. "I figured since I couldn't take you there, I'd give you an exotic name to remind me to keep striving for more. And someday, I'd get to London. You were my inspiration."

Londyn nodded. "And you made it."

"Yes, I did. And when I went..." she looked up at Ben, "I couldn't stop thinking about our honeymoon."

Nash walked with Londyn back to the house.

As they climbed the steps to the porch, Londyn stopped and turned to stare out at the landscape bathed in brilliant starlight. "I hate leaving."

As Nash stood behind her, he wrapped his arms around her waist and drew her close. "Then don't go."

She tipped her head back, resting it against his chest. "I have to do this."

His arms tightened around her. "You realize the danger still exists."

She nodded. "Which makes me even more determined to see this through. Nobody is going to scare me off the set or force me off my property." She stiffened against him and turned in his arms. "If they want a fight, I'm ready to give it to them."

Nash's lips curled upward. "You're amazing. Other women would've given up on the ranch and making that film." He brushed a strand of her hair back from her forehead, then bent to touch his lips there.

"Is it too forward of me to ask if you'd like to do a repeat of last night?" she whispered.

He chuckled. "No and no."

Her brow puckered. "No?"

"Not a repeat. I'd rather not camp out in the barn like we did last night." He held up a hand. "Don't get me wrong. It was incredible."

Her fingers walked up his chest. "Can I interest you in a bed?"

He leaned his forehead against hers. "Always."

She took his hand and led him up the stairs and into her room, closing and locking the door behind them.

His gut told him the next few days back in Yellowstone would be challenging. But for that night, all Nash wanted to think about was Londyn, holding her in his arms and making love to her.

They undressed each other and lay on the bed, their bodies entwined, cuddling until cuddles weren't enough. The fire of desire ignited quickly, consuming them in flames. They made love until nearly midnight. Afterward, Londyn nestled in his arms, her naked body pressed to his, her breathing slowing as she fell into a deep, restful sleep.

Nash lay awake a lot longer, mulling over everything that had happened that day and worrying about going back to the movie set.

He needed to touch base with Swede. By now, the tech guru should have some information from his background checks.

When they returned to Yellowstone, Nash wanted to keep a close eye on Craig Ryland. The man had blatantly lied to the director about Londyn quitting her job.

Why? What did he hope to gain?

Unless Craig wanted Londyn off the set so he could get the leading lady of his choice on the project.

Londyn had been the only person targeted out of all the other actors. Since being back on her ranch, no attempts had been made on her life. It all boiled down to her involvement in the movie. Someone didn't want her there and wouldn't stop until she was off the set permanently by forcing her to quit.

Or eliminating her altogether.

Yeah, sleep wouldn't come easily.

CHAPTER 15

THE ALARM JARRED Londyn awake in the early hours of the morning.

Nash pulled her close and held her for a long moment.

She loved the way his skin felt against hers and how her body molded perfectly to his. "I wish we could stay here all day," she whispered.

"Me, too," he murmured. "But we have to move if we want to get to the set before they start filming."

"Yeah." Londyn sighed, drew in a deep breath and stretched.

Nash rolled out of the bed and stood, his gorgeous body kissed by the remaining starlight streaming through the window.

Heat coiled at Londyn's core. "Do we have time to—"

He grinned and shook his head. "If we start, I

won't be able to stop. We'll miss our departure time and have to explain to your mother why."

Londyn grimaced and pushed to her feet. "You can have the bathroom first. I'm still questioning my existence."

"I won't be long," Nash jammed his legs into the jeans she'd secured for him and padded out the door barefooted.

Londyn dressed quickly in nice trousers, a rib-knit blue sweater and, of course, her boots. She had just started smoothing the tangles out of her hair when Nash stepped through the door.

He crossed to take the brush out of her hand and gently worked through the tangles until all were gone and her hair was smooth and silky.

She turned in his arms and leaned up on her toes to kiss him. "You could hire out your hair-brushing skill and make a fortune."

"I reserve that skill for special people." He kissed the tip of her nose. "The bathroom is all yours."

Though she'd rather stay in the circle of his arms, Londyn hurried out of the room and into the bath-room. Minutes later, with her face washed and her teeth brushed, she was ready to go.

They descended the stairs to find her mother standing at the bottom, a robe wrapped around her, her face free of makeup. She enveloped Londyn in a tight hug. "No matter the mistakes I've made along the way, know that I love you and only ever wanted you to be happy."

"I love you, too, Mother." Londyn leaned back. "Are you staying here for a while?"

Her mother nodded. "I think so. I have unfinished business I need to tend to."

Londyn cocked an eyebrow. "Namely, Ben Standing Bear?"

Her mother's cheeks flushed with color. "After all these years apart, I didn't think I'd have any feelings left for him." She laughed. "I was wrong."

Londyn hugged her again. "Life is short. You have to follow your heart."

"I asked one of the ranch hands to drive you out to the plane," her mother said. "He's waiting in the truck."

Londyn left the ranch house, her heart a little lighter, knowing her mother was still there and that she might finally get her happily-ever-after.

The ride to the plane didn't take long. It stood on a dirt landing strip used by local crop-dusting pilots.

She climbed up into the small plane, settled in a seat and buckled her safety harness.

Nash dropped into the seat beside her and buckled up. They pulled headsets over their ears and listened for instructions from the pilot.

Soon, the plane was taxiing down the hard-packed dirt runway, gathering speed. Moments later, the wheels left the ground, and they were in the air, heading south to Yellowstone.

Nash had called Dan Mitchell at the T-Bar-M Ranch the night before and asked for the closest landing strip to the movie set at Yellowstone. Mitchell had offered the dirt strip on his ranch and added that he'd be happy to transport them from there to the Yellowstone location.

The roar of the aircraft's engines and the use of headsets limited casual conversation.

Londyn calmed her nerves by looking out the window at the plains below them and the snow-capped Rocky Mountains in the distance. She was incredibly lucky to live in such a beautiful area of the country and hoped she never took it for granted.

The drive that had taken four hours took a mere hour in the plane. They landed as the first gray lights of dawn brightened the sky.

As promised, Mitchell was waiting for them in his truck, and he'd brought food.

"Cookie heard I was picking you two up before dawn and insisted on sending breakfast burritos." He handed Londyn a small cooler. "There's orange juice in there as well, or you can have the coffee in the thermos." He nodded toward the thermos in the front seat.

"Coffee," Londyn moaned and handed the cooler to Nash. She poured steaming brew from the thermos into the empty cups positioned in the truck's cup holders.

After Londyn capped the thermos, Mitchell shifted into drive. "I got word from Dr. Matheson. He was able to get the test results quickly. They found traces of amphetamines in the blood sample."

"Amphetamines?" Londyn shook her head. "You mean she didn't eat something bad?"

"Not unless she got a hold of a bottle of amphetamines lying around," Mitchell said.

"Which means someone gave her the drugs," Nash said.

Heat rose up Londyn's chest and neck into her cheeks. "I can put up with being the target of some asshole trying to kill me, but they better not fuck with my horse."

Mitchell shot a glance her way. "Someone is trying to kill you?"

Nash explained the damaged props and explosives that destroyed her trailer.

Londyn set her coffee cup back in the cupholder to prevent it from spilling. Her hand shook too much from the anger burning through her. "And now, they've attacked my horse."

"That's some serious shit," Mitchell said. "Are you sure you want me to take you back to the movie set? Sounds too dangerous to me."

"I'm going back," she said, her jaw tight, her nostrils flaring. "Now that my horse is safe at home, it's game on. I'll find who's responsible, and I promise I'll make them pay."

Londyn spent the remainder of the drive to the film location in brooding silence, planning all the ways she'd hurt the person making her life and horse's life miserable.

When Nash offered her a burrito, she declined. Her stomach was roiling at the thought of someone drugging her horse.

Thankfully, she had enough time on the drive to cool down. By the time they reached the movie set, her heart rate had returned to normal, but her determination to find and destroy the person behind the attacks was set in stone.

When Mitchell pulled into the parking area, the sun had risen, and people were already at work, manning cameras, adjusting lighting and positioning props.

Londyn dropped down from the truck and shook hands with Mitchell. "Thank you for all your help. If you're ever in my area of Montana, my door is always open to you," she said. "I'd love to have you visit."

"I hope you find the snake in the grass," Mitchell said.

Londyn's eyes narrowed. "Oh, we will."

Mitchell glanced toward the set. "The ground should dry within a couple of days. I'll see you when they come to shoot the cattle drive." He climbed into his truck and lowered the window. "I look forward to seeing your movie. I can't wait to say I knew you when." He grinned, pulled out of the parking area and headed back to his ranch.

Londyn squared her shoulders and marched toward the set.

The cameras were positioned around the barn. Director Haynes stepped back, out of view of their lenses, and yelled, "Action!"

Craig and Troy acted out the fight scene Londyn's character Lana was supposed to break up.

Julia Banes burst onto the scene in Londyn's costume, her black curls straightened. Dark foundation makeup covered her face and hands.

Londyn strode into the middle of the scene, at which point the director yelled, "Cut!"

"Oh, sorry," she said, touching her fingers to her lips. "Were you filming?"

"Damn right, we were," Haynes groused. "Why are you here? I thought you quit."

Londyn gave him a tight smile. "If I quit, you'll know I quit because I would tell you."

Haynes, brow furrowed. "What else was I do believe? I was told you quit yesterday."

"Who told you that I quit?" Londyn asked.

Haynes looked around as if trying to remember. His gaze landed on Craig and Julia. He frowned at them. "You two were the last ones to get back from the T-Bar-M Ranch. It was you who told me she wasn't coming back, wasn't it?"

Craig frowned. "Yes. Julia was the last person to talk with Miss Tyler-Lovejoy as they were leaving yesterday morning. She was shocked that Londyn changed her mind at the last minute and said she wouldn't be coming back to the set and that she wanted us to let you know." He shook his head. "I was shocked as well after Londyn told me that she planned to come back after she got her horse home. I was going by what Julia said. What reason would she have to lie?"

Julia's eyes widened. "I wasn't lying. I swear Londyn told me she'd changed her mind. Maybe I heard her wrong, but I thought that's what she'd said."

Londyn shook her head. "Our last conversation was you telling me our director called to let us know we'd be on a three-day hiatus to let the sets dry out. I specifically said I could be available as soon as they started filming again. Nowhere in anything I said did I say I was quitting."

Julia raised her hands, palms up. "I'm sorry if I got the message confused."

Director Haynes glared at both actresses. "I don't care who said what. Time is money, and we're burning through both." He pointed to Julia. "Give the costume to Londyn."

"She has no acting experience," Julia said. "The only reason she's here is because she's Dana Tyler's daughter."

"Costume. Now," Haynes said, his voice low and angry.

"You want the clothes?" Julia said. "Take them." She kicked off the boots, unbuttoned the trousers and shoved them down her legs. Then she whipped the blouse over her head and flung it at Londyn. "When this film flops, you'll only have yourself to blame." She turned and stalked away in her bra and panties.

None of the cast or crew said a thing. Like Londyn, they were likely stunned by Julia's dramatic exit.

Haynes's eyes narrowed as his gaze followed her off the set. "We'll have a discussion later about your actions and your contract," he called out, then turned and pointed at Londyn. "You have twenty minutes to get into costume, hair and makeup."

"What scenes are we working on?" Londyn asked.

Haynes glanced at the clipboard in his hand. "We'll shoot the fight scene again, then we have the big cabin fire."

Londyn hadn't had time to practice her lines for the fire scene. She'd only have the time it took for hair and makeup artists to work their magic to figure it out. If she remembered correctly, there weren't many lines in that scene, just action.

When Londyn hesitated, Haynes snapped his fingers. "Go!" He glanced around. "Someone give hair and makeup the heads-up." His assistant hustled off to find the ladies in charge of hair and makeup.

Londyn gathered the garments Julia had thrown on the ground and looked around. With no trailer to change in, she headed for the cabin.

Nash fell in step beside her. "Do you need help getting ready?"

"No, but I need a copy of the script. I left mine in my truck at the ranch." She glanced around. "Do you remember the trailer where I got the last copy?"

He nodded.

"If you could get that for me, it'll save me from going there and give hair and makeup more time to work on me."

Nash frowned. "I don't want to let you out of my sight."

"Then find someone who can get it for me." She stopped in front of the cabin. "Right now, I have to change."

"After I check inside." He opened the cabin door, stepped inside and was back out a few moments later. "It's empty. I'll be right back."

"I'll be here," she said with a smile. She started to enter the cabin, changed her mind and caught his arm. "Thanks for being here for me." Londyn leaned up and brushed her lips across his. "I'm getting used to having you around."

He caught her around her waist, crushed her to

him, wad of clothes and all, and claimed her lips. "I like being around," he said. "I'll be right back."

"I'm counting on it," she said a little breathlessly. She went into the cabin as Nash spun and hurried away in search of someone to run her errand.

With just minutes to make it happen, Londyn stripped, pulled on the costume designed for the barn fight scene and shoved her feet into the boots.

She was shoving her own clothes into a drawer in the prop cabinet when the door to the cabin opened behind her.

"That was fast," she said as she turned toward Nash.

Only it wasn't Nash standing in the doorway. It was one of the ground crew who helped with a variety of jobs, including moving equipment into position, adjusting lighting and managing props.

She frowned. "Do you need to adjust a prop in here or something?"

He nodded without speaking. His vibe was...unsettling.

Londyn gave him a stiff smile. "I was just leaving."

As she started for the door, the man stepped in front of her.

"Excuse me," she said. "I need to be on set in ten minutes."

The door behind him opened.

Londyn breathed a sigh of relief. Nash would handle this guy.

When Julia entered the cabin, Londyn's relief was short-lived.

She frowned when she saw Londyn and then said to the props guy, "What are you waiting for? We don't have much time."

"I need to get back to the set," Londyn said with as much false confidence as she could muster. Her gut was telling her that shit was about to go down. "Do you think you can get this guy to move out of my way?" She had to stall them from whatever they had in mind until Nash returned. He said he'd be right back. Where was he?

"If you're looking for your boyfriend, you can forget about him." Julia's lip curled back in a sneer. "He won't be coming to your rescue this time."

CHAPTER 16

Nash didn't like leaving Londyn for even a minute. And just when he needed to find someone, everyone was busy getting equipment in place. He'd only gone maybe thirty yards when his cell phone chirped, indicating an incoming text. He fished it from his pocket and glanced down to see the message was from Swede.

> Look out for Alan Sarley, hired on with the film studio as maintenance. Dishonorable discharge from the Marines for spousal abuse even after mandatory anger management therapy.

Nash started to respond when his cell phone rang. The name on the screen was Dana Tyler. He answered, "Yes, ma'am."

"Nash, I checked into the other women who audi-

tioned for the lead role Londyn landed. Only one
made the cut but was awarded the role of supporting
actress instead of the lead."

"Let me guess," he said. "Julia Banes?"

"That's the one," Dana said. "I had my agent check
into her background. She's got a reputation for being
hard to work with. A real diva."

"I'll keep an eye on her," Nash promised.

"Thanks." Dana hesitated. "How's my girl?"

"She's getting ready for her next scene," he said.
"Gotta go."

"Take care of her," Dana said.

"Yes, ma'am." Anxious to get someone to find a
script, he ended the call.

As he pocketed his cell, he heard someone shout,
"Look out!"

Nash looked up in time to see the heavy lighting
fixture he was standing near teeter precariously and
then topple in his direction.

The man who'd shouted rushed toward him.

"Don't!" Nash yelled and dove for the man,
knocking him backward. The metal fixture crashed
down, pinning Nash and the man he'd shoved
beneath its heavy frame.

For a moment, Nash's vision blurred. He fought
the darkness. He couldn't pass out. He needed to get
back to Londyn.

As Nash's vision cleared, pain shot through his leg

and shoulder. He tried to move. The weight of the equipment trapped him against the ground.

The man he'd shoved muttered a string of curses and then asked between gritted teeth, "You all right, man?"

"Can't...move," Nash said, the weight of the fixture smashing him into the dirt and making it hard to breathe. He pushed his hands against the ground and tried to push up.

"Hang on," the other guy said. "Let me try. It's only got my leg pinned." The man grunted and cursed. "No use. We're going to need a hand." He raised his voice. "Hey! Help!"

A voice answered back, "Coming!" Soon, a man came running up. "Holy shit, Brody! Gonna need more than me. I'll be right back."

"Hurry," Nash said into the dirt.

"Max'll get help," Brody said. "What's your name?"

"Nash," he replied.

"Nash, you the guy with our leading lady?" Brody asked.

"Yes," he replied. "Need...to...get...back..."

"Here they come. They'll get us out of here," Brody said. "Just hang on."

Nash struggled to get enough air in his lungs to keep from passing out. He counted the seconds, his gut telling him he needed to hurry.

He was up to one hundred seconds when Max returned with four other guys.

Four men positioned themselves on opposite sides of the structure and gripped the metal struts. The fifth man stood close to Nash.

"On three," Max called out. "One...two...three!"

The men all lifted as one.

As soon as the weight was off him, Nash sucked in a deep breath. The man standing near him grabbed his arm and pulled him from beneath the metal.

Nash looked toward the other guy who'd been trapped beneath the wreckage.

Brody had dragged himself out from under the fixture.

By the time the four men had lowered the structure, others came running from all over.

"I called 911," one man said. "They're sending an ambulance."

Nash struggled to his hands and knees.

Someone laid a hand on his shoulder. "Hey, buddy, you should stay down until the paramedics get here. You could have some damage to your back."

Nash shook his head. "Just help me up." He had to get to her. As he searched the faces standing around, he didn't find Julia's. And he wasn't sure what Alan Sarley looked like.

With each passing second, he was more and more convinced Londyn was in danger.

His heart raced, and his breathing became labored and not from the weight of the metal crushing him into the earth. A flashback of Waterson filled his memories, and he knew how that had ended.

He wouldn't let that be how things went down this time. Not with Londyn. Not on his watch.

LONDYN WORRIED about what Julia and her giant-sized minion had done to Nash. She had to know. The man she'd tried to get rid of at first had proven himself to be a true hero. The kind of man most women could only dream of.

In the short time they'd been together, he'd managed not only to save her life twice, but he'd also gotten under her skin.

As she'd learned the hard way, when you loved someone, you held on as long as you could and loved them with every fiber of your being. Life could be fleeting. She had to treat every day like it could be her last. And she wanted to spend every one of them with that annoying man who'd insisted on protecting her when she'd believed she could take care of herself.

"What did you do to Nash?" she asked, praying they'd been bluffing when they'd said he wouldn't be coming to her rescue.

"Let's just say we knocked his lights out," Julia said, her lips curling in a feral smile. "We wouldn't have had to if you'd just gone into your trailer when you were supposed to."

"So, you set the charges and tampered with the props?"

"Alan, here, loves to make a big splash. You're all about the drama, aren't you, my love?"

Alan slipped an arm around Julia's waist without replying.

Londyn's eyes narrowed. "Which one of you poisoned my horse with amphetamines?"

Julia practically purred. "You were the one who insisted on bringing your own animal to the game, I knew that if something happened to it, you'd get angry and leave. I was right—and from what I heard, you almost drowned getting her back." The bitch tsked her tongue. "Such a shame your boyfriend was there to pull your ass out of the water. Again, this," she waved her hand at the interior of the cabin, "wouldn't be happening if you'd just die. What are you? A cat with nine lives?"

Londyn's lips pulled back in a snarl. "You nearly killed my horse. I swore I'd find the person who did that and make him pay. And if you hurt Nash, I swear I'll take you down."

"Now then, that will be kind of hard to do if you're not around." Julia's mouth formed a thin, hard line. "Enough talk. We don't have much time." She glanced at Alan and jerked her head toward Londyn. "You know what to do."

With only one way out of the cabin, Londyn figured she couldn't dodge her way out. More than likely, she'd have to fight her way out. If she could get past the muscle-bound asshat, she could easily take the bitch down.

"You know, we'd all have been happier if you'd just stayed on your little ranch in Montana. You'd be home with your horse, and I'd have the part I deserved in the first place."

Alan took a step toward Londyn.

She tensed and waited until he got closer, putting a little distance between himself and Julia.

When he lunged for her, Londyn shot to the right, ducked around him and almost made it to Julia.

Alan swung around, grabbed a handful of her hair and yanked her backward.

Londyn fought like a wild cat. She kicked, punched and even bit the man. But he was bigger, stronger and quickly subdued her by throwing her on the ground and crushing her with his body.

Julia produced a roll of duct tape and wrapped some around Londyn's ankles. Once she had them secured, Alan leaned back, gripped both of Londyn's wrists and pulled them behind her back.

Julia wrapped tape around them. She tore off a short piece and slapped it over Londyn's mouth. She straightened and looked down her nose at Londyn as she lay on her side on the floor of the cabin.

"The charges are set?" Julia asked Alan.

He nodded.

"Let me hold the detonator while you move her to the center of the room." She held out her hand.

Alan dug in his pocket and pulled out a small device. He handed it to Julia and then grabbed Londyn by the ankles and dragged her across the floor.

Londyn bunched her legs and tried to kick the man in the shins. He backed out of reach.

Julia stood behind the man with a crowbar in her hands. She raised it above Alan's head and slammed it down with all the force of a lumberjack splitting wood.

When the iron bar hit Alan's head, it made a loud cracking sound.

Alan crumpled to the floor and lay still.

"The man was great in bed but dumb as a rock. This way, I can tie up all the loose ends and get back to my trailer before anyone knows or can do anything about it." She smiled and held the device up in her hand. "You really shouldn't have taken the part. I had it before your mother interfered." She slid the safety off the device and pressed the button. "Happy trails."

A small explosion erupted beneath the cabin, shaking the floor beneath Londyn's cheek.

Julia tossed the detonator onto the floor near Londyn, smiled and walked out the door.

Londyn tried to scream while the cabin door was open, but the tape over her mouth muffled her cries.

Smoke filtered through cracks in the floor beneath her.

Londyn's heart raced. The explosion had to be the incendiary device set up for the cabin fire they were supposed to shoot later that day. Since the cabin was made of wood, it would be fuel for the fire and be consumed quickly.

Londyn had to get out of there or die of smoke inhalation or be burned alive in the flames.

She looked around the cabin for anything she could use to cut through the duct tape on her wrists. Her heart plummeted to the pit of her belly when she couldn't find anything sharp enough to do the job. No jagged metal. No butcher knives. Nothing.

If she could get to the door, perhaps she could pull it open.

With her hands bound behind her back and her ankles locked together, she moved across the floor by rolling her entire body and inch-worming until she reached the door.

Once there, she tried reaching the doorknob with her feet. Her boots hindered her ability to turn the knob. She tried hooking her boots over the top and pulling them off, duct tape and all, but the binding was too tight, and the boots weren't budging.

The smoke thickened quickly.

Londyn rolled onto her belly and planted her forehead against the floor. Trying to maintain her balance, she hiked her butt into the air and pulled her knees up beneath her and rose to a kneeling position. At this point, she was eye-level with the doorknob and no nearer to opening the door.

She'd be damned if she died staring at the door she couldn't open. There had to be a way.

Londyn leaned her head against the door and rocked backward in an attempt to get on her feet.

She rocked back all right, lost her balance and fell onto her back, smacking her head against the floor.

No. No. No. I will not let that bitch win.

Flames ate through the floor near the rear of the little cabin. Though the smoke rose, it was quickly filling the ceiling space and edging closer to the floor where Londyn lay.

Now would be a good time for people to notice the cabin was on fire and come check to see if anyone, namely Londyn Tyler-Lovejoy, was inside.

Once they noticed the fire, they'd come running. Londyn just had to make enough noise to alert them to the fact there was someone trapped inside. She prayed for help while rolling close to the door. Keeping her head as close to the floor and breathable air as she could, she kicked the door.

Her grandfather had taught her the Morse code for SOS. What was it again?

She kicked three short taps, three long and three short.

Not that it made a difference. If they saw the fire

and heard banging, surely they wouldn't try to read the code before breaking down the door.

All she knew was to keep kicking and praying.

Please, Nash, be okay. Come save me one more time. Three's a charm, right?

NASH FOUGHT the pain in his back and leg, forcing himself to stand upright. He moved his arms and legs. Though they hurt, they worked. He didn't think anything was broken.

As he turned, he smelled smoke.

"Fire!" someone yelled.

Even before he saw it, he knew it would be...

The cabin.

"Fuck, fuck, fuck." Nash shuffled one foot at a time, his muscles resisting every step of the way. He felt like he was in one of his nightmares where he couldn't run because his legs were bogged down in swamp mud.

The more he pushed himself, the faster he moved until he was sprinting toward the cabin. As he neared, he heard banging from within.

When he reached the cabin, the banging had stopped. He tried opening the door, but the knob wouldn't turn. "Londyn!" he yelled.

Another softer bang sounded against the door and stopped.

"Move away from the door!" he yelled.

Nash backed a step away, cocked his leg and kicked as hard as he could.

The door frame made a splitting sound but held.

He kicked it again, and the door opened halfway, bumping into something on the floor.

Smoke poured out, hitting Nash in the face and burning his eyes.

He ducked low and pushed against the door, moving whatever was blocking it until he could see inside.

The lump blocking the door was a body.

Nash's heart leaped into his throat.

He dove through the door, immediately blinded by the smoke. Feeling along the floor, he found her, grabbed her arm and pulled her through the door.

Once he had her out of the building, he scooped her up in his arms. He carried her away from the burning building and the smoke billowing from inside before he laid her on the ground and gently removed the tape covering her mouth.

Immediately, she started coughing.

Nash helped her sit up. He dug out his pocketknife and sliced through the tape wrapped around her wrists and ankles and then pulled her into his arms. "I'm sorry," he said, burying his face in her smoky hair. "I'm so sorry."

In between fits of coughing, she said what sounded like, "Three's a charm."

He wasn't sure what that meant and didn't really care. She was alive.

When she could stop coughing long enough, she pointed to the cabin. "Did they get...Alan...out?"

"They did," a voice said behind Nash.

Nash turned to find the director, Steven Haynes.

"We didn't get him out in time."

Londyn shook her head. "He was dead... before the smoke."

Haynes frowned. "How?"

"Julia hit him..." Londyn burst into another coughing fit before she could finish with, "crowbar."

"Julia did this?" Haynes shook his head.

"Don't let her...get away...with murder." Londyn coughed again and leaned against Nash's shoulder.

Haynes face hardened. "We'll take care of it. And just so you know, we're putting production on hold until you're well enough to come back to work."

Londyn gave the director a weak smile. "Thanks."

Haynes stared down at her. "I didn't hire you because of your mother. I hired you because you were exactly who we needed to portray Lana. So, hurry back. We can't do this movie without you."

Within fifteen minutes, an ambulance arrived. The paramedics got Londyn on oxygen and stabilized her until a rescue flight arrived to take her to the hospital in Bozeman.

Nash stayed with her, insisting on accompanying her on the helicopter. He almost started a fight in the

ELLE JAMES

ER when they refused to let him go back with her because he wasn't a relative.

One call from Hank Patterson, and he was immediately allowed to go back with Londyn. When they moved her to a private room to monitor her overnight, he was with her the entire time.

Haynes sent him a text to let him know Julia had been arrested for the murder of Alan Sarley and the attempted murder of Londyn.

Nash should have rested easier knowing the woman wouldn't hurt Londyn ever again. But he didn't sleep at all that night, plagued by an irrational feeling that if he closed his eyes, something awful would happen.

By sunrise, he was almost delirious with the exhaustion of the trauma to his body and his soul. He'd come so close to losing Londyn, making him realize that not only did he like her, but he had also fallen head over heels in love with her.

As daylight filled the room, Londyn stirred, opened her eyes and smiled up at him.

His heart melted. "Your smile just brightened my world." His vision blurred as moisture filled his eyes.

Londyn frowned up at him. "Hey," she said, her voice not much more than a gravelly whisper. "Did you think I was going to let that bitch get away with poisoning my horse?"

He laughed for the first time in what felt like

forever. "No way in hell. When you make a promise, I can count on you to keep it."

Londyn lifted her head off the pillow. "They did catch Julia, didn't they?"

Nash nodded. "She was arrested for murder and attempted murder."

Londyn laid back and closed her eyes. "Good. I can't say that I'm sad she killed Alan. He set the explosives and sabotaged the props. But Julia was the one who poisoned Buttercup. I hope she rots to death in prison."

A knock sounded on the door.

Sadie McClain peeked her head around the door. "May we come in? It's okay if you're not feeling up to it. We won't bother you."

"No, please, come in." Londyn tried to sit up and push her hair out of her face. "I must look awful."

Sadie crossed to the side of the bed, carrying a vase of pink and white carnations. "Oh, sweetie, don't you worry about it. After what you've been through, it's a miracle you survived. Hank told me you nearly drowned and almost died in a fire. I told him you should come to White Oak Ranch to let me take care of you while you recuperate."

Londyn laughed. "I can't even imagine what it would be like to have Sadie McClain waiting on me hand and foot."

"Sorry, but she needs to be in her own home, surrounded by family who will take care of her."

Nash turned to find Dana Tyler and Ben Standing Bear standing at the door to Londyn's room.

"Mother?" Londyn looked around Hank and Sadie.

Dana walked around to the other side of the bed and took her daughter's hand. "Hey, baby."

"How did you get here so quickly?"

Dana tipped her head toward Nash. "Your young man called me when they admitted you to the hospital yesterday. Ben brought me over in his airplane today." She shook her head. "Did you know he has his private pilot's license?"

Londyn looked from her mother to Ben. "No, I didn't."

"Like I was saying," Dana said. "You can recuperate at home on the ranch. I'll be staying indefinitely if that's all right by you."

Londyn smiled at Hank and Sadie. "Thank you for the offer. Though I'd love to visit sometime, I'd really like to be home." She turned to Nash. "As long as you come home with me."

Nash's heart swelled. "Wild horses couldn't keep me away." He looked around the room at Hank, Sadie and Dana. "I want to thank you all for having the confidence in me to provide protection for Londyn. Without this opportunity, I wouldn't have met Londyn and found out what a strong, courageous and loyal woman she is. And beautiful." He grinned. "Did I say beautiful?" His smile slid away. "But I can't accept your money for this job. Because you see, I would do it for free and for the rest of my life." He laughed.

Hank, Sadie and Dana all shook their heads.

"I'd pay ten times what we agreed on," Dana said. "You saved my daughter's life."

"Three times a charm," Londyn murmured.

Nash shot a glance toward Londyn. She'd said the same thing when she'd been half out of it after he'd pulled her out of the burning cabin.

Dana held up her hands and backed away. "I won't let you refund my money."

"You heard the client," Hank said with a grin. "Your first assignment as a Brotherhood Protector was a success. If you don't want to be paid, you can donate that amount."

"I know of a woman's shelter," Sadie said. "They always need food, supplies and scholarships for women trying to get themselves out of abusive situations."

"Donate it," Nash said.

"Done," Hank said.

"Hank," Nash squeezed Londyn's hand gently, "if you don't want me to work for you anymore, I'll understand."

Hank chuckled. "Nash, you're exactly the kind of person we want as a Brotherhood Protector. I don't accept your resignation if that's what you're doing.

After Miss Tyler-Lovejoy recuperates, we'll have another assignment waiting for you."

Nash nodded. "Thank you, sir."

Sadie set the vase of flowers on a table. "Hank, we should go. I promised Chuck and Kate we'd be back early enough that they can hit Taco Tuesday at the Blue Moose Tavern. It's their date night." She smiled at Londyn. "I'm glad you're going to be all right, and I know you'll spring back in no time because that's what badass women like you do. Hank and I can't wait to see the movie when it comes out. We'll be at the premiere to cheer you on. And, please, come see us."

"Thank you so much for everything," Londyn croaked, her voice fading by the end of the sentence.

Hank and Sadie left the hospital room.

Londyn's mother leaned over and hugged her daughter. "I know I haven't always been the best mother, but I've always loved you. It broke my heart to let you go live with your grandfather. I didn't want you to move further away from me, but knowing you were happier and more in your element on the ranch made it an easier pill to swallow." She straightened. "I hope you can forgive me someday for not telling you about your father."

Londyn's eyes filled with tears. "Already have," she whispered.

Tears slipped down her mother's cheeks. She hugged Londyn again and then stepped back.

Ben Standing Bear moved to the side of the bed and lifted Londyn's hand. "We've all made mistakes in our lives and lost years because of them. We can't make up those years, but I hope we can take advantage of those we have left. I want to get to know you, Londyn, as my daughter and as a friend."

Londyn squeezed his hand, tears slipping from the corners of her eyes.

Nash could only imagine the emotion behind those tears. The years she'd missed knowing a father who'd been close by all along. He thought of how lucky he'd been to have a stepfather who cared enough to make him feel as much a part of his family as his own little girls.

Londyn's mother and father left.

Londyn's gaze followed them out the door. When it closed behind them, more tears slipped down her cheeks. She turned to Nash and held out her hand.

He went to her, took her hand in his and raised it to his lips. She held onto him with one hand and patted the bed with her other.

Careful not to disturb the IV, Nash laid on the bed beside her, slid his arm beneath her neck and molded her body to his.

"Stay with me?" she whispered.

He tightened his hold. "Now and forever, if you'll have me."

She closed her eyes and smiled. "Yes, please."

EPILOGUE

EIGHTEEN MONTHS LATER...

"Beautiful," Sadie McClain dabbed at the corner of her eye. "I wouldn't be surprised if you and the movie are nominated for an Oscar." She hugged Londyn.

Londyn stood outside Grauman's Chinese Theater on Hollywood Boulevard, dressed in an elegant Versace-designed dress. At first, she'd refused to wear the gown when she'd learned how much it cost.

Her mother had bought the gown anyway. "You wouldn't let me help you pay off the ranch debt, so the least you can do is let me splurge on the dress," her mother said. "You might as well wear it. It's paid for, and they don't allow returns. It was made for you and would be a crime against fashion to never be photographed. Think of wearing it as an advertisement for the talented artists who designed it and the talent actress wearing it."

Standing beside Nash, surrounded by the people she loved, Londyn felt beautiful and happier than she'd ever been. And she had a secret she'd been carrying close to her chest for the past week that made her even happier.

She stared at her husband of six months. He wore a black tuxedo, complete with cummerbund and bowtie. The man was stunning. And he was hers, body and soul.

With all the press time, talk show interviews and preparation for the movie's release, she hadn't had time to tell him her secret. Neither of them had been home on the ranch for much of the past two months. When they were together, they spent a lot of time in bed, making love, laughing and just being together.

Nash had only just returned from an assignment that had taken him to London for a week.

"Sweetheart," Londyn's mother hurried toward her, her face glowing with pride. "The movie's premiere is a huge success. Everyone who attended is raving about the story, the cinematography and your stellar portrayal of Lana." She hugged her daughter so hard Londyn could barely breathe. "I'm so proud of you, darling."

"Thank you, Mother," Londyn said, her heart brimming with happiness. "That means a lot to me."

Her mother stepped back. "Did you get the contract for the sequel?"

Londyn nodded.

"And?"

"Nash and I discussed it." Londyn glanced toward her husband. "We agreed that I should do it. But I asked to push the start date out another six months, giving me a year and a half to get ready."

Her mother's brow wrinkled. "Why would you need a year and a half to get ready?"

"Yeah," Nash frowned, "why do you need a year and a half to get ready? You're in terrific shape and more beautiful than ever."

"He's right," her mother said. "You're practically glowing. As you should, with your first movie a huge success."

Sadie McClain moved closer. "You are glowing with more than pride for a job well done." Her eyes widened, and a smile spread across her face. "You're pregnant," she said softly. "Oh, Londyn, I'm so happy for you and Nash."

"Wait," Nash shook his head. "What?" He turned toward Londyn and gripped her hands, his brow dipping low on his forehead. "Pregnant? Really?"

"I wanted to tell you tonight...in private," she squeezed his hands, her heart bursting with joy.

He shook his head, his eyes wide. "With a baby?"

Everyone laughed, including Londyn.

"That's usually how it works." Hank clapped his

back. "Congratulations, Nash. You're going to love being a father."

Nash's face split in a huge grin. "I'm going to be a father."

Londyn laughed. "Yes, you are. We're going to have a baby."

Everyone gathered around to congratulate them.

Nash pulled Londyn into his arms and kissed her so gently it made her heart melt all over again.

Nash leaned his forehead against hers. "I love you, Londyn, and I can't imagine life without you. I can't wait to share that life with our baby."

"I love you, too," she said. "I didn't know I was missing out on so much until I met you." She cupped his cheek in her hand. "Then you came along and filled all the empty spaces and so much more. Thank you for insisting on protecting me when I tried to push you away. I can be stubborn."

He kissed the tip of her nose. "It's one of the things I love most about you." He slipped an arm around her. "Come on. We have an afterparty to go to and so many reasons to celebrate."

She walked with him into the rest of her life.

ATHENS AFFAIR

BROTHERHOOD PROTECTORS
INTERNATIONAL BOOK #1

New York Times & *USA Today*
Bestselling Author

ELLE JAMES

INTERNATIONAL
ATHENS AFFAIR

New York Times & USA Today Bestselling Author
ELLE JAMES

CHAPTER 1

HIRING on with the Jordanian camera crew as their interpreter hadn't been all that difficult. With Jasmine Nassar's ability to speak Arabic in a Jordanian dialect and also speak American English fluently, she'd convinced the Jordanian camera crew she had the experience they needed to handle the job. However, the resume she'd created, listing all the films she'd worked on, had probably lent more weight to their decision.

Not that she'd actually worked on any movie sets. Her ability to "be" anything she needed to be, to fit into any character or role, was a talent she exploited whenever needed since she'd been "released" from the Israeli Sayeret Matkal three years earlier.

Her lip curled. Released was the term her commanding officer had used. *Forced out* of the special forces unit was closer to the truth. All because of an affair she'd had with an American while she'd been on holiday in Greece. Because of that week in Athens, her entire life had upended, throwing her into survival mode for herself and one other—her entire reason for being. The reason she was in Jordan about to steal the ancient copper scroll.

The Americans arrived on schedule for the afternoon's shoot at the Jordan Museum in Amman, Jordan. The beautiful film star Sadie McClain appeared with her entourage of makeup specialists, hairstylists, costume coordinators, and a heavy contingent of bodyguards, including her husband, former Navy SEAL Hank Patterson.

Sadie was in Jordan to film an action-adventure movie. All eyes would be on the beautiful blonde, giving Jasmine the distraction she'd need to achieve her goal.

Much like the movie heroine's role, Jasmine was there to retrieve a priceless antique. Only where Sadie was pretending to steal a third-century BC map, Jasmine was there to take the one and only copper scroll ever discovered. The piece dated back to the first century AD, and someone with more money than morals wanted it badly enough he'd engaged Jasmine to attain it for him.

Up until the point in her life when she'd been driven out of her military career, she'd played by the rules, following the ethical and moral codes demanded by her people and her place in the military. Since the day she'd been let go with a dishonorable discharge, she'd done whatever it took to survive.

She'd been a mercenary, bodyguard, private investigator and weapons instructor for civilians wanting to know how to use the guns they'd purchased illegally to protect themselves from terrorist factions like Hamas.

Somewhere along the way, she must have caught the eye of her current puppet master. He'd done his homework and discovered her Achilles heel, then taken that weakness in hand and used it to make her do whatever he wanted her to do.

And she'd do it because he had her by the balls. He held over her head the one thing that would make her do anything, even kill.

Her contact had timed her efforts with the filming of the latest Sadie McClain blockbuster. The museum was closed to the public that afternoon but was filled with actors, makeup artists, cameramen, directors and sound engineers.

The American director had insisted on an interpreter, though Jasmine could have told him it was redundant as nearly half the population of Jordan spoke English. Part of the deal they'd struck with the Jordanian government had been to employ a certain percentage of Jordanian citizens during the production of the movie. An interpreter was a minor concession to the staffing and wouldn't interfere with the rest of the film crew.

Plus, one inconsequential interpreter wouldn't be noticed or missed when she slipped out with the scroll in hand.

For the first hour, she moved around the museum with the film crew, reaffirming the exits, chokepoints and, of course, the location of her target. She'd visited the museum days before as a tourist, slowly strolling through, taking her time to examine everything about the building that she could access, inside and out.

The scroll was kept in a climate-controlled room away from the main hallways and exhibits. Since the facility was closed to the public, there wouldn't be anyone in the room.

While the crew set up for a scene with Sadie McClain, Jasmine slipped into the room to study the display cases once more.

The copper scroll had been cut into multiple pieces. Each piece had its own display case with a glass top, and each was locked. She'd brought a small file in the crossbody satchel she carried, along with a diamond-tipped glass cutter in the event the locks proved difficult. Cutting glass was the last resort. It would take too much time and could make too much noise if the glass shattered.

She'd honed her skills in picking locks and safe-cracking as a child, one of the many skills her mother had taught her. She'd insisted Jasmine be able to survive should anything ever happen to her parents.

Her mother had been orphaned as a small child in the streets of Athens. To survive, she'd learned to steal food and money, or valuables that could be sold for cash or traded for food.

From picking pockets and swiping food from stores and restaurants, she'd worked her way up to stealing jewelry, priceless antiques and works of art from the rich all around the Mediterranean. She'd used her beauty and ability to quickly learn new languages to her advantage, infiltrating elite societal circles to divest the rich and famous of some of their wealth.

She'd gone from a starving, barefoot child, wearing rags in the streets of Athens, to a beautiful young woman, wearing designer clothes and shoes and moving among the who's who of the elite.

Her life had been what she'd made of it until she'd met Jasmine's father, a sexy, Israeli Sayeret Matkal soldier, at an Israeli state dinner attended by wealthy politicians, businessmen and their wives. She'd just stolen a diamond bracelet from the Israeli prime minister's wife.

The special forces soldier outfitted in his formal uniform had caught her with the diamond bracelet in her pocket and made her give it back as if the woman had dropped it accidentally.

Rather than turn her in for the theft, he'd kept her

close throughout the evening, dancing with her and pretending she was just another guest.

Her mother had fallen for the handsome soldier and agreed to meet him the next day for coffee. Less than a month later, they'd married.

For love, her mother had walked away from her life as a thief to be a wife and mother. But she'd never forgotten the hard lessons she'd learned on the streets. She'd insisted her daughter learn skills that could mean the difference between independence and dying of starvation or being reliant on someone who didn't give a damn about her health or happiness.

Her mother had taught her what school hadn't, from languages, dialects and staying abreast of the news to learning skills like picking locks, safe cracking, picking pockets and hacking into databases for information. She'd learned skills most parents didn't teach their children or warned their children to avoid.

Jasmine had earned her physical capabilities from her father. As an only child, she'd been the son her father never had. As an elite Sayeret Matkal, her father had kept his body in top condition. Jasmine had worked out at home with him and matched his running pace, determined to keep up with the father she loved so fiercely.

He'd taught her how to use a variety of weapons and the art of defending herself when she had no weapons at all. Because of her dedication to conditioning, her hand-to-hand combat skills and her ability to speak multiple languages, when she'd joined the Israeli military, she'd been accepted into Sayeret Matkal training soon after.

After the Athens affair and her subsequent release from the elite forces, she'd continued her training.

Now, due to circumstances out of her immediate control, she was on the verge of stealing from a museum the priceless copper scroll the Jordanians were so proud of.

Her jaw hardened. If she had to steal every last item in the museum, she would—anything to get Eli back alive.

She pulled the file from her satchel, glanced toward the room's entrance and then bent to stick the file into the little keyed lock. She fiddled with the lock until she tripped the mechanism, and the lock clicked open.

Jasmine tested the case top by lifting it several inches and then easing it back down. One down, several more to go. She'd work them a few at a time. When she had all the locks disengaged, she'd take the scroll and walk out of the museum or leave with the Jordanian film crew.

She cringed at the thought of waiting for the crew to head home. They could be there well into the night, filming take after take until they perfected the sequences.

No, she'd head out as soon as she could. She had a deadline she would not miss—could not miss—if she wanted to see Eli again.

Jasmine jimmied the locks on a few more of the displays and then returned to where the crew was staging the next scene with Sadie McClain.

In the shadow of a statue, one of Sadie's bodyguards shifted, his eyes narrowing. He wore a baseball cap, making it difficult to see his face.

Something about the way he held himself, the line of his jaw and the dark stubble on his chin struck a chord of memory in Jasmine. A shiver of awareness washed over her. She hurried past him without making eye contact.

When she looked back, the space where he'd been standing was empty.

Jasmine shook off a feeling of déjà vu and stood near the Jordanian camera crew, interpreting when needed but basically remaining quiet and out of the way.

With the preparations for the big scene complete, the camera crews stood ready for the director to shout *action*.

All other personnel were to move out of the line of sight of the cameras. This gave Jasmine the opportunity to slip back into the room with the copper scroll. When she heard the director shout, *"Action,"* Jasmine went to work quickly and efficiently, lifting the tops off the glass cases one at a time, wrapping each piece of the copper scroll in a soft swatch of fabric she'd brought in her satchel, handling them carefully so as not to break the fragile copper.

Jasmine placed each piece inside a box she'd designed specifically for transporting the delicate scroll. Once all the pieces were stored, she closed the box and slid it into her satchel.

Taking the extra time, she returned all the tops of the glass cases to their original positions so they wouldn't draw attention until a museum employee just happened to notice the cases were empty. That should buy her time to get the items out of the museum and out of Jordan before anyone became suspicious.

With her satchel tucked against her side, Jasmine hurried out of the room. At that moment, the director yelled, "Cut!" He motioned to the film crews and gave orders to the American and Jordanian cameramen.

Some of the Jordanians looked around for their interpreter.

Ready to get the hell out of the museum, Jasmine had no choice but to approach the cameramen and provide the necessary translation for the director. All the while, her hand rested on her satchel, anxiety mounting. The longer she stayed in the museum, the greater the chance of someone discovering the copper scroll was missing.

Short of racing out of the building and drawing

attention to herself, she remained, forcing a calm expression on her face when inside she was ready to scream. A life depended on her getting out of the museum and delivering the scroll—Eli's life.

ACE HAMMERSON—HAMMER back in his Navy days— thought he recognized the interpreter as soon as she'd stepped through the museum doors with the Jordanian camera crew. The more he studied her, the more he was convinced it was her.

Jasmine.

The woman with whom he'd spent an amazing week in Athens. A week he could never forget.

Had it really been four years?

Granted, she looked different from the last time he'd seen her. She'd changed. Her dark hair peeked out from beneath the black scarf she wore over her head and draped around her shoulders. Her curves were hidden beneath a long black tunic and black trousers. Her face was a little thinner, but those full, rosy lips and her eyes gave her away. There was no mistaking the moss green irises that had captivated him from the first time he'd met her at an outdoor café in the Monastiraki district of Athens.

He'd come to Antica Café on a recommendation from a buddy who'd been there a year earlier. The place had been packed, with no empty tables left. Tired and hungry after the twenty-hour journey from San Diego to Athens, he'd just wanted to eat, find his hotel and crash.

Rather than look for a less crowded café, he'd looked for an empty seat. A beautiful woman sat in a far corner, a book in her hand, enjoying a cup of expresso. Ace had approached, hoping she wouldn't blow him off, and asked if she spoke English.

She'd looked up at him with those amazing green eyes and smiled. In that moment, he'd felt a stirring combination of lust, longing and... strangely...homecoming wash over him. It could have been exhaustion, but more than hunger made him want to join this woman at her table.

She spoke English with a charming accent he couldn't place as either Greek or Arabic. When he'd asked if he could share her table, she'd tilted her head and stared at him with slightly narrowed eyes before finally agreeing with a relaxed smile.

That had been the beginning of the most incredible week of his life. His only regret was that he'd had to go back to work after that week. Before he'd had time to look her up, based on the phone number she'd given him, he'd deployed for several months to Afghanistan, where the mission had been so secret, they'd gone incommunicado to avoid any leaks.

By the time he'd returned to his home base, her number had been disconnected.

He hadn't known where to begin looking for her. In all their conversations, she'd barely revealed much about her life other than both her parents were dead, having been killed in a Hamas strike in Israel.

Because of her reference to her parents being killed in a Hamas strike, he'd assumed she was from Israel. She'd talked about her mother having been from Greece and her father from Israel. Like him, her father had been on vacation in Athens when he'd met her.

Ace had searched for her online, hoping to find out something about her whereabouts, but failed miserably. On his next vacation, he'd gone back to Greece, to the same restaurant where they'd met, hoping by some strange coincidence he'd find her there. He'd walked the same paths they'd walked through the city, looking for her. He'd stayed in the same hotel where they'd stayed, even insisting on the same room.

She hadn't been there. He'd gone to Tel Aviv and talked with some acquaintances he'd met during joint training exercises with the Israeli military. They hadn't heard of her.

As many people as there were in Israel, Ace hadn't expected to find her just by asking around. But he'd hoped that the same magic that had brought them together the first time would help him find her again. After a year, he'd admitted defeat and tried to forget her.

That had never happened. Every woman he'd dated after Jasmine had never sparked in him the fire and desire he'd felt with the woman he'd met in Athens.

Now, here he was, freshly out of the military, working with Hank Patterson and his team of Brotherhood Protectors in Amman, Jordan. Nowhere near Athens and four years after that fated affair, she walked back into his life.

New to the Brotherhood Protectors, Ace had agreed to accompany Hank and members of his team to Jordan to provide security for the film crew and actors who were friends of Hank's wife, Sadie McClain, on her latest movie set. He'd be an extra, there to observe one of the team's assignments.

They didn't always provide security for film crews, but since significant unrest existed in the countries surrounding the relatively stable Jordan, the film producers and studio had budgeted for a staff of security specialists.

Hank had worked with the studio and cut them a deal to ensure his people provided security for his wife and the crew there to make movie magic. Brotherhood Protectors were the most qualified to provide the safety net they might need if fighting spilled over the borders from countries surrounding Jordan.

Though he'd been excited and curious about the mechanics of making a movie, Ace's attention had shifted the moment Jasmine entered the museum.

His gaze followed her as she moved among the Jordanian film crew, standing between Americans and Jordanians, interpreting instructions when needed.

As the camera crew set up, Jasmine left them to wander around the museum, looking at ancient artifacts on display. At one point, she disappeared into a side room and remained gone for several minutes.

Ace started to follow when Hank approached him. "It's amazing, isn't it?"

Ace nodded. "Yes, sir."

Hank grinned. "I never imagined the amount of people it takes to produce a film until I accompanied Sadie on set for the first time."

Though Ace would rather focus his attention on Jasmine's movements, he gave his new boss all his attention. "I never realized there was so much involved."

"Right? It takes an incredible amount of coordination to set up a gig like this, from securing a location to getting permission, in this case, from the government to film here, to transporting all the equipment. Not to mention hiring people to do all aspects, including lighting, sound, video, makeup and costumes."

Ace's gaze remained on the door through which Jasmine had disappeared. "And that's just the filming," he commented, mentally counting the seconds Jasmine was out of his sight.

Then, she emerged from the room and rejoined her camera crew.

Ace let go of the breath he'd been holding.

Hank continued the conversation Ace had lost track of. "After the filming, there's the editing, music, marketing and more." The former Navy SEAL shook his head, his lips forming a wry smile. "I have so much more respect for all those names that scroll across the screen in the movie theater when they show the credits." He chuckled. "I always wondered, and now I know, what a key grip is."

Jasmine worked with the cameramen once more, then stepped back into the shadows.

Once the cameramen were in place, the lighting guy gave a thumbs-up. The director nodded, spoke with Sadie and then stepped back.

"They're about to start filming," Hank said.

When the director raised a hand, everyone grew quiet.

The director looked around at the placement of the cameras, Sadie and the lighting, then nodded.

Ace felt as though everyone took a collective breath, waiting for it...

"Action!" the director called out.

Ace's attention was divided between Jasmine, the actors, the cameramen and the supporting staff.

The beautiful, blond actress, Sadie McClain, did not command his attention like Jasmine.

Sure, Sadie was gorgeous, dressed in khaki slacks that hugged her hips, boots up to her knees and a flowing white blouse tucked into the narrow waist-band of her trousers.

Her mane of golden hair had been styled into a natural wind-swept look with loose waves falling to her shoulders. She worked her way through the museum corridor, pretending to be a patron until she arrived at a golden statue encased in a glass box.

As Sadie studied the statue, her character assessing her chances of stealing it, Jasmine slipped out of the main museum corridor into the side room again

What was she doing in there?

Ace wanted to follow her, but to do so, he'd have to pick his way through the camera crews and lighting people. He didn't want to get in the way while the cameras were rolling. God forbid he should trip over a cable, make a noise or cast a shadow and make them have to start all over again.

So, he stood as still as a rock, all his attention on that room, counting the seconds until Jasmine came out or the director called, "Cut!"

Finally, Jasmine emerged from the room.

At the same time, the director yelled, "Cut!"

The crossbody satchel she'd worn pushed behind her now rested against the front of her hip; her hand balanced on it. Her head turned toward the museum entrance and back to the organized chaos of camera crews shifting positions and responding to the director's suggestions. An American cameraman approached the Jordanian crew and spoke in English.

Members of the Jordanian camera crew frowned, looking lost. One of them spotted Jasmine and waved her over.

Jasmine's brow furrowed. Her gaze darted toward the museum entrance once more before she strode across the floor to join the cameramen. She listened to the American cameraman and translated what he was saying for the Jordanians, who, in turn, grinned, nodded, and went to work adjusting angles.

Jasmine stepped back into the shadows.

Ace nodded to Hank. "Excuse me. I want to check on something."

Hank's eyes narrowed as his gaze swept through the people milling about. "Anything to be concerned about?"

Was there anything to be concerned about? Ace's gut told him something was off, but he didn't see a need to alarm Hank until he had a better idea of what. "No, I just want to look at some of the displays."

"Are you a history buff?" Hank asked.

"A little. I'm always amazed at artifacts that were created centuries much earlier than our country's inception."

Hank nodded. "Yeah, some of the items in this museum date back hundreds of years before Christ."

He gave Ace a chin lift. "Explore while you can. It looks like they're getting ready for another take."

His gaze remained on Jasmine as Ace strode across the smooth stone floors to the room Jasmine had visited twice in less than an hour.

The room was climate-controlled, with soft lighting and several display cases positioned at its center. At a brief glance, nothing appeared out of place, but as Ace moved closer to the display cases, he frowned. They appeared...

Empty.

His pulse leaped as he read the information plaque beside the row of cases.

COPPER SCROLL. 1ST CENTURY AD.

He circled the cases and found that they all had keyed locks. He didn't dare lift the tops off the cases. If he did, he'd leave his fingerprints all over the glass and possibly be accused of stealing what had been inside.

His stomach knotted. Jasmine had been in here. Had she come to steal the copper scroll? Did she have it stashed in that satchel she'd carried around all afternoon?

Ace spun on his heels and left the room. His gaze went to the last place he'd seen Jasmine. She wasn't there.

His pulse slammed into hyperdrive as he scanned the vast corridor where the film crew worked.

She was nowhere to be seen.

Ace strode toward the museum's entrance. As he neared the massive doors, someone opened the door and slipped through it.

That someone was Jasmine.

What the hell was she up to? If she'd stolen the scroll, he had to get it back. If he didn't, the museum would hold Hank's team responsible for the theft, especially considering they were the security team.

The copper scroll was a national treasure. If he didn't get it back, it could cause an international incident as well as delay film production.

Ace slipped out of the museum and paused to locate the thief.

Dark hair flashed as Jasmine rounded the corner of a building across the street from the museum.

Ace had to wait for a delivery truck to pass in front of him before he could cross the road. As he waited, two large men dressed in black entered the side street, heading in the same direction as Jasmine.

Once the delivery truck passed, Ace crossed the street and broke into a jog, hurrying toward the street Jasmine had turned onto.

As Ace reached the corner of the building, he heard a woman shout, "No!"

He turned onto the street.

A block away, the two men in black had Jasmine by her arms. She fought like a wildcat, kicking, twisting, and struggling while holding onto the satchel looped over her neck and shoulder. One man ripped the scarf from her head and reached for the satchel's strap.

"Hey!" Ace yelled, racing toward the men.

Jasmine used the distraction to twist and kick the man on her right in the groin. When he doubled over, she brought her knee up, slamming it into his face.

The injured man released her arm.

Jasmine turned to the other man, but not soon enough. He backhanded her on the side of her face hard enough to send her flying.

As she fell backward, the man grabbed the satchel and yanked, pulling it over her head as she fell hard against the wall of a building.

Clutching the satchel like a football, the man ran. His partner staggered to his feet and followed.

Ace would have gone after them but was more concerned about Jasmine.

The men ran to the end of the street. A car pulled up, they dove in, and, in seconds, they were gone.

Jasmine lay against the wall, her eyes closed, a red mark on her cheek where the man had hit her.

Anger burned in Ace's gut. He wanted to go after the men and beat the shit out of them. But he couldn't leave this injured woman lying in the street.

He knelt beside her and touched her shoulder. "Jasmine."

Jasmine moaned, blinked her eyes open and stared up into his face, her brow furrowing. "Ace?

What—" She glanced around, her frown deepening. "Where am I?" She met his gaze again. "Is it really you?"

His lips turned up on the corners. "Yes, it's me. You're in Jordan." His brow dipped. "You were attacked."

She pinched the bridge of her nose. "What happened?"

"Two men attacked you," he said.

"Two men..." She shook her head slowly. "Jordan..." Then her eyes widened, and she looked around frantically. "My satchel! Where is my satchel?"

"The men who hurt you took it."

She struggled to get to her feet. "Where did they go? I have to get it back." As she stood, she swayed.

Ace slipped an arm around her narrow waist. "They're gone."

"No!" She raked a hand through her hair. "I need that satchel." Jasmine pushed away from Ace and started running back the way they'd come, then stopped and looked over her shoulder. "Which way did they go?"

He tipped his head in the direction the men had gone.

When Jasmine turned in that direction, Ace stepped in front of her and gripped her arms. "They're gone. You won't catch up to them now."

"Why didn't you stop them? They stole my satchel!" She tried to shake off his grip on her arms.

His lips pressed together, and his grip tightened. "What was in the satchel, Jasmine?"

"Something important. I have to get it back. Please, let go of me."

"Was the copper scroll in your bag?" he asked quietly so only she could hear his words.

Her gaze locked with his. For a moment, she hesitated, as if deciding whether or not to trust him. Then she nodded. "I had to take it. If I don't get it back, someone I care about will die."

ABOUT THE AUTHOR

ELLE JAMES also writing as MYLA JACKSON is a *New York Times* and *USA Today* Bestselling author of books including cowboys, intrigues and paranormal adventures that keep her readers on the edges of their seats. When she's not at her computer, she's traveling, snow skiing, boating, or riding her ATV, dreaming up new stories. Learn more about Elle James at www.ellejames.com

Website | Facebook | Twitter | GoodReads | Newsletter | BookBub | Amazon

Or visit her alter ego Myla Jackson at mylajackson.com
Website | Facebook | Twitter | Newsletter

Follow Me!
www.ellejames.com
ellejamesauthor@gmail.com

Made in the USA
Monee, IL
28 May 2024